THE LADY'S GAMBLE

ANNE R BAILEY

Inkblot Press

Copyright © 2021 by Inkblot Press

All rights reserved.

No part of this book may be reproduced in any form or by any electronic or mechanical means, including information storage and retrieval systems, without written permission from the author, except for the use of brief quotations in a book review.

Any references to historical events, real people, or real places are used fictitiously. Names, characters and places are products of the author's imagination.

ALSO BY ANNE R BAILEY

Forgotten Women of History

Joan

Fortuna's Queen

Thyra

Royal Court Series

The Lady Carey

The Lady's Crown

The Lady's Ambition

The Lady's Gamble

Bluehaven Series

The Widowed Bride

Choosing Him

Other

The Stars Above

You can also follow the author at: www.inkblotpressco.ca

Plainly I cannot glose;
>   Ye be, as I divine,
>   The pretty primrose,
>   The goodly columbine.
>   With marjoram gentle,
>   The flower of goodlihead,
>   Embroidered the mantle
>   Is of your maidenhead.

Benign, courteous, and meek,
>   With words well devised;
>   In you, who list to seek,
>   Be virtues well comprised.
>   With marjoram gentle,
>   The flower of goodlihead,
>   Embroidered the mantle
>   Is of your maidenhead.

—John Skelton, *The Garland of Laurel*

CHAPTER ONE

"At least my wits will sharpen with age. The same cannot be said for your supposed beauty." Elizabeth stormed out of the queen's chambers. Her heart beat wildly in her chest as she made her way to her brother's rooms.

She could not believe she had said that, and to Lady Hastings too! She rounded the corner, weaving around the courtiers in the corridors as she replayed what had happened in her head.

Her sister had not lifted a finger to help her, even though she was queen and could have settled the matter with one word. The longer she thought about it the more her temper flared. At least Edward would listen to her if no one else would.

She barrelled past the guard posted at her brother's door in his brown and yellow livery. Edward was inside at his writing desk, while Anne Stanhope, his wife of a year, lounged on a chaise by the fire. They both looked up at her with mild surprise.

"She's infuriating," Elizabeth said, with a small bob to them both. "I hope you are both well," she added, remembering to try to be courteous.

Edward invited her to sit, but she shook her head. She was too on edge to contemplate taking a seat.

"You would think Lady Hastings would have more respect for the queen's sister, but apparently not," Elizabeth said, seeing that Edward was waiting for her to speak. The ghost of a smile on his face disappeared.

"She was disrespectful?"

"That wasn't even the half of it, and Jane just sat there looking pleased with herself and oblivious to everything." Elizabeth crossed the room in a few long strides, her hand massaging the back of her neck to ease the growing tension. She hated the heavy gable hoods her sister had reintroduced at court.

Lately, it felt like everything Jane did was to punish her. Everyone thought Jane, with her meekness and pale complexion, was a simpleton. If Elizabeth didn't know Jane better, she would have agreed and never dreamed her sister would be so devious. But she knew better.

"You are making me dizzy with your pacing," Anne said.

"Gather your thoughts and tell me what happened," Edward suggested.

"No, it's fine. I let my emotions get the better of me and I overreacted. You know I can handle myself in most situations. But Anne Hastings commented on my children and it made my blood boil. I may have implied she was dim-witted." Elizabeth bit her lower lip to keep herself from laughing. Now that she was out of the situation she could afford to be amused.

"She shouldn't be making comments like that to the sister of the queen." Edward was frowning.

His wife scoffed from her chair. "Jane hardly makes an imposing queen."

The scorn in her voice was hard to miss. Elizabeth wouldn't be surprised if she, along with nearly every other lady at court, thought she would have had a better chance of snaring King Henry than Jane did. She wasn't pretty, she wasn't talented, so why had he chosen her?

"She knows more than she lets on, but that doesn't matter. This will reflect poorly on me," Elizabeth said.

"You care too much what other people think," Edward pointed out.

Elizabeth shot Edward a look but took a seat across from Anne. She sank into the seat of the newly upholstered chair. It was pointless to argue with Edward. He couldn't understand what it was like being a woman. Your worth was derived from what people thought of you. Unless you were fabulously rich—then you could afford to buy yourself a position in society and the good opinion of anyone.

"At least I got the last word in." Elizabeth smiled to herself, toying with the fringe of lace at her sleeve. "At the very least they will see that not all Seymours are simpering simpletons."

Edward chided her. "You should make up with Jane. It would not do to have our family divided."

"If she showed me an ounce of kindness, I would consider it. I don't understand why she shows me such contempt," Elizabeth said.

"You are letting your emotions get the better of you. I am sure you have considered exactly why Jane has been cold to you..." He paused, smiling as he recognized the expression on her face. "So it has crossed your mind. Well, you are not incorrect. You are the younger, prettier, fertile sister made suddenly available on the marriage market. It will take her some time to stop seeing you as a threat. Then you will be perfect friends again. It doesn't matter if you never so once looked the king's way. Jane was threatened by you."

Elizabeth felt her throat clench in disgust.

Her son and daughter were in the care of their grandfather. As an impoverished widow, she did not have any claims on their wardship. She had no say in any aspect of their lives. Their grandfather was kind enough to allow her to visit them, but her dearest desire was to have them back in her keeping.

Elizabeth had come to court hoping to find some way to make this happen. Surely, now that her sister was queen, this should have been an easy feat. She didn't have time to think about fetching another husband, much less one from underneath her sister's nose. If her sister took a moment to think it through, she would see that. But at the moment her sister had very little compassion for her. She was scared, and rightfully so. The throne on which she sat was still warm from its previous owner, whose life had ended with the swing of a sword.

She blinked when a goblet of wine was thrust toward her. The blood-red liquid sloshed over the edge, some spilling on her fingers and threatening to spill on her one good gown.

"You look like you need it more than I do," Anne said.

Elizabeth thanked her with a grim smile and sipped. It was of the best quality. She glanced around her brother's rich rooms. Everyone had benefited to some extent except herself.

"You will be fine in the end. You always are." Edward placed a hand on her shoulder. "Jane will learn what it is to rule. We will be at her side, nudging her along."

She could only nod in reply.

Perhaps Jane did not have the influence over the king she ought to have, but Elizabeth had hoped that Jane would speak to him on her behalf.

Of course she had been greeted with resentment and suspicion. Edward was right. However, once it clicked in her sister's head that she wasn't here to supplant her place, they could be friends again. They weren't Boleyns after all. Jane would come to her aid.

"There's also the issue of Jane feeling unsteady on her throne. She's been acting imperious." Anne broke the silence. "She's been aloof with her ladies-in-waiting. Apparently, we aren't good enough for her."

"I have noticed that. It's probably why she's desperate to have Pr—Lady Mary back at court." Elizabeth had to stop herself from calling Mary princess. It slipped every once in a while. Princess Mary had been declared a bastard four years ago, and it was now treason to call her princess. "I mean, it must also be getting annoying to have Chapuys dogging your steps."

That earned her a laugh from Edward, but he stopped when he saw his wife's warning look.

He coughed into his sleeve and moved around to her side.

"We must be respectful toward Chapuys. He was one of the men that helped us."

"Yes, we were fortunate to have his assistance. What do you think he will do if we can't deliver?" Elizabeth was looking from her brother to Anne.

"There's nothing he could do or accuse her of." Anne waved a hand dismissively.

"We've seen first-hand that the truth does not matter. We better ensure that our sister the queen can accomplish what we promised on her behalf. Otherwise, we will fail just like the others that came before us." She handed back the half-empty goblet to a gaping Anne.

Edward's barking laugh broke the gloom that had set upon the room.

"She's not wrong." He lifted his own glass to Elizabeth in a toast. "To my sister's quick mind, may it never dull." He downed the wine in one big gulp.

Anne looked up at him as though she might scold him, but she held her peace.

Elizabeth felt herself relax. She let go of her frustration with each breath. She had to remember that there was more at stake now.

"So, Lady Anne, was it you who decorated these rooms?"

"Yes, I did a little moving around of the furniture here and there. I ordered a few tapestries to be brought from Wolf Hall, and I've commissioned two others."

Anne was content to talk on about such trivialities for over an hour. Elizabeth did her best to humour her. Edward had drifted away to his writing desk, eager to leave them to their discussions.

She would have to return to the queen's apartments. The sun was dipping on the horizon, and they would be getting Jane ready for bed. It would be noticed if she did not return.

Without much enthusiasm, she thanked her brother and his wife for their company.

"I am grateful for your hospitality. That wine was delicious. French?"

"English."

"Of course." Elizabeth's knowing smile slid over the pair. All things French went out of style with the Boleyn queen.

The privy chambers were abuzz with activity. The ladies running back and forth might have seemed like chaos to a stranger, but it was an organized procedure. Some ladies brought the bed linen while others laid it out. Others were clearing away the odds and ends from the day's sewing or other activities. Some were helping Jane to undress while the others started the process of bathing her. The king was visiting. He had visited her every night since their marriage. Elizabeth did not believe he was solely driven by passion for her pallid sister. He wanted a son to prove to the world he'd been right to put aside one queen and behead another, only to marry and try again.

Every morning and night she added a little prayer that Jane would succeed where others had failed. Despite the bad blood between them now, she did not wish her to come into harm's way. A son. All they needed was for Jane to have a son.

Her head held high, she strode over to her sister, who seemed engulfed by the other ladies—more a ghost than a queen.

"Shall I plait your hair, Your Grace?" she asked, taking a comb from a maid.

Jane gave her a curt nod.

She always seemed on edge in the evenings. Elizabeth knew she had always been shy, so to suddenly be surrounded by people during what was usually a private event must be hard on her.

She unpinned Jane's blond hair, so light it was almost white in the correct light. It came tumbling down her back. Elizabeth was careful to hand over each gold pin studded with pearls to a waiting attendant. These could not be haphazardly misplaced. Each one was worth the yearly salary of a page boy.

Taking the comb in one hand and a chunk of hair in the other, she began the arduous task of detangling the mop of hair.

"Did you have a pleasant day?" Elizabeth said, keeping her tone soft and soothing.

"Yes." The reply had seemed forced, but Jane continued. "It was lovely riding out in the morning. I have never seen a sky so blue before."

"Hmm."

They talked like this a while longer. The others seemed to be happy to let them lead the conversation, keeping to banal topics.

"All done," Elizabeth said at long last.

Jane had a moment in which she looked panicked, and Elizabeth felt the urge to take her hand and ask her what was wrong. But of course nothing could be wrong. She was the luckiest woman in all of England. No, the world.

"Do I have time to pray?" Jane looked to one of the senior ladies who had just handed her a furred robe to throw over herself.

The lady looked a bit taken aback. How could she know when the king would arrive? After a moment's pause, she nodded. "You should have time, Your Grace."

She watched as Jane all but ran for her prie-dieu. A pang of sympathy for her shot through Elizabeth. She wanted to walk over to her and ask her what was wrong. However, that would accomplish nothing. Everyone in this room knew what she was praying for as she knelt in front of the altar, the prayer beads digging into her palms. There was no turning back for her, but would she collapse inwardly from the stress of it all?

Unable to stand it, Elizabeth drifted over to her, kneeling down beside her.

"Sister, I am here for you. If you need me, Your Grace."

Jane did not speak but nodded, never taking her eyes off the Virgin Mary.

"You will be strong and you will accomplish all you set out to do," Elizabeth reasserted, hoping they looked like two ordinary sisters praying together, not ones having secret conversations.

"I will," Jane said, crossing herself. She stood, seeming to have steeled herself, a hand grazing her belly as though searching for any signs of a life growing inside.

She had stood not a moment too soon. The king's herald stepped into the room to announce his arrival. Elizabeth got to her feet but disappeared behind the other ladies. She had no desire to stand out.

Jane stood by the great bed, her back straight. No one would notice that anything was wrong, except she had tied the belt of her robe too tightly.

He came strutting into the room, scanning the faces of all the ladies as he did so, a smile to each as they bobbed up and down in their curtsies until his gaze settled on Jane, waiting.

"I bid you good night, my sweetheart."

She bowed her head. "I pray you are well, my lord husband."

He smiled benignly.

Elizabeth could see his gentlemen of the privy chamber move to investigate the bed. A sword was carried in, and she couldn't take her eyes off it as a man took it and plunged it into the feather mattress.

In moments like these it was clear that while the king played at being brave, he was truly paranoid as well.

In one swift motion the sword was pulled out, filling the room with the sound of whistling steel. Elizabeth wondered if that was the last sound Anne Boleyn had heard before she met her grisly end. She couldn't stop herself from replaying the scene over and over in her head. She had not been there to witness it for herself, but she had heard plenty of tales.

The king waved his hand after the priest had blessed the bed. They were dismissed.

Everyone began drifting away from him, not turning their backs to him as that would be seen as rude. Elizabeth chose to wait outside her sister's apartments for the king to leave. He rarely slept beside her sister throughout the night but retired to his own rooms. Everyone knew but dared not comment.

She waited outside the rooms, flipping through a prayer book and trying to avoid the gaze of Richard Rich staring at her from across the room.

He was one of Cromwell's men.

A man who came up from nowhere. She knew that men like her brother feared these nobodies. They had circumvented tradition and had risen above their station. They were a threat and made the nobility obsolete. Of course, her family had used these upstarts to help get their sister on the throne. It was with Cromwell's help that the first queen was divorced and the second toppled off her throne. So it was Cromwell who had placed Jane in her current position.

She stole a quick glance in Rich's direction. Ever observant, he had caught her movement and flashed her a smile. Elizabeth looked back to her book. Not wanting to insult him, but neither did she want to invite conversation with this man. To her, men working for Cromwell had proven to be unscrupulous and untrustworthy. How could anyone trust a spy?

However, he was also currently a member of the king's privy chamber. A favoured companion with intimate access to the king's person. His position was enviable and gave him a lot of influence.

It would not do to upset a man like him.

She prayed he would grow bored.

Her eyes drifted to the Italian clock on the mantel. How long would this take? They weren't completely alone, as other members of the queen's household came and went about the room. Elizabeth feigned great interest in their comings and goings. She watched as the fireplace was cleared of soot and new logs were placed inside.

She hoped her sister was well.

Her thoughts were interrupted by Richard's voice.

"You seem to have done well away from court. Are you planning on staying or heading back to Wolf Hall?"

She hated his presumption in talking to her, even more so that he thought she would share her plans with him.

Elizabeth looked over to him with a bored, cool

expression she hoped would put him off any further conversation.

"I have not decided."

"Surely you have some inclination. Perhaps you are looking for a new husband?"

She had to fight hard to keep her composure and not let her discomfort show on her face. Were all "new men" this forward? Even if she was, it was not up to her to get married, nor would negotiations proceed so fast and openly.

"I see I have stumbled on a touchy subject. I should excuse myself."

"Then why don't you?" She couldn't help but snap back. This little show of temper seemed to amuse him.

He stood, stretching his arms toward the ceiling. It was such an unusual action to do in front of her. Overly familiar.

She looked away from him, hoping he would get the hint. She wasn't here to befriend a person from nowhere, of no social standing. The only claim he could make was that he was one of the king's favourites.

"Cromwell doesn't appreciate your family's recent standoffishness. Perhaps you can pass that message along to your brother, Edward. That title he now holds was a gift, and it can easily be taken away again. Don't forget who put you where you are."

His voice was like a hiss in her ear.

He was standing closer to her now so they wouldn't be overheard. Perhaps he thought he was being menacing, but he was failing. Up close, he was a man growing portly around the middle with a receding hairline and beady dark brown eyes.

"If you have a problem with my brother, you better take it up with him. I am not about to get in the middle of whatever this is."

She fixed him with one of her more haughty expressions. Hoping the anger and annoyance radiating off her would hide her fear from him.

He looked surprised but pleased.

"I am glad to find you are nothing like your sister."

"And what do you mean by that?" She couldn't help herself from asking.

"Well, you actually have fire in your belly. The phoenix should be your emblem, not hers."

Elizabeth felt a twinge of pleasure at the compliment, but it wasn't like she could be bought so easily. She looked away.

This time he seemed content to leave her alone.

At length, the king emerged from her sister's rooms looking pleased with himself. Though he walked with a more obvious limp now.

He clapped a hand on Richard's back as though to congratulate himself. Elizabeth took this time to slip back into the room without being noticed.

Jane was still in bed, buried under the heavy covers. She was holding herself still, her eyes closed as though in prayer.

Elizabeth tried not to look her way, knowing how private her sister was and not wishing to disturb her.

She went around the great bed to the sideboard.

Finding a plate of sweetmeats and a jug of ale inside, she poured it into a waiting cup.

As quiet as any mouse, she tiptoed to the blazing fireplace and took a hot poker, mulling the ale.

As the satisfying sizzle died down, she put the poker back and approached the silent figure.

A pale hand shot out from beneath the covers, reaching for the cup.

"You will have to sit up," Elizabeth warned.

"I won't move for a while longer." Her voice sounded cracked, as though she had been intent on silence.

"Why?"

"I was told it would help..." The words hung in the air. Elizabeth had to choke back a laugh. She wanted to tease her sister. She couldn't possibly be listening to all the old tales and bedside gossip.

"He already talks of the son growing in my womb. But how can I know for certain there is one? How can he?"

Elizabeth sighed, knowing she had no answer for her sister.

Jane grabbed her around the wrist.

"What will he do if I am not with child?"

Pulling her arm free, Elizabeth tried to reassure her. "He will wait. You may be blessed, but I am sure he does not truly expect it of you. Never show any doubts about your fertility. If there isn't a child now, there will be later. Your marriage is good in the sight of God, you are young, no one in your family has had trouble in this regard. Remind him of this."

Jane seemed reassured somewhat. She propped herself up and drank deeply. The warm drink returned some colour to her skin.

"Remember, worrying yourself so much will only make things worse. Be happy."

"Everyone tells me I am the luckiest woman in the world." Her sister's dry tone made her laugh.

"Aren't you?"

"Oh, I am," Jane assured her, but her expression told a different story.

Their courtly masks disappeared as they grinned, sharing a knowing smile and a laugh at the irony of the situation.

Elizabeth felt a twinge of love for her older sister.

There was some hope now that their bond could be reforged. And even if it was a lost cause, she had to help keep Jane steady on her feet. Their family's fortunes rose and fell with her.

Elizabeth would not let her fall.

She had drifted back to her own rooms that she shared with Madge Shelton. Elizabeth would have preferred not to room with Madge, who had a certain reputation about the court.

It had surprised her to find so many of Anne Boleyn's old attendants serving Jane, but it was clear that her sister had very little say in the matter.

At least Anne's fall from grace had tempered

Madge's brazen behaviour. She was even sporting the conservative English gabled hood.

Personally, Jane missed the French fashions that were lighter and kept her head cooler in the summer months, but she wasn't about to argue.

This morning they were going to travel to Greenwich from Whitehall by barge. The king had planned a full day's entertainment centred around it. They were all decked in their best. The barges would be decorated with garlands of flowers, and musicians would play. There were even rumours of a firework display. This was all in Jane's honour.

Elizabeth arrived early, as she had not slept well the night before. She was standing in the courtyard, adjusting her worn-in gloves, when she heard heavy footsteps coming up behind her.

She craned her head to see who it was and caught sight of Arthur Darcy approaching.

She bit the inside of her cheek, trying to school her features into determined indifference. She had seen him a lot at Wolf Hall when he came with his father, though he spent most of his time with her brothers. Arthur came from a respectable family in the north and, more importantly, his father held a wealthy barony in Lincolnshire.

He was only the third son, however, and unlikely to inherit much. He would have to marry well to make his fortune. Despite this, he had seemed keen on pursuing her, and not with the noblest of intentions either.

She had almost been grateful when her father had announced her engagement, knowing that she would be free of his attention. She hadn't considered that he might also be back at court. But she should have known—after all, where else could one catch wealthy heiresses in his net?

"Lizzy, I am surprised to find you here," he said, taking off his cap and bowing to her. It was an exaggerated gesture meant to flatter her.

She could not be rude and turned to him with a strained smile.

"I have not been at court long, Lord Arthur." She hoped he would take her hint and continue the conversation in a more formal manner, but that did not seem to be his intention.

"Fate always seems to bring us together. I thought I had lost you forever to that godforsaken island in the middle of nowhere."

"It is hardly surprising, given that my sister is queen now. I expect I will be seeing a lot of my old acquaintances."

"Ah, but we are more than just mere acquaintances. We have history."

She stepped back, as he had slid closer. She knew his game. If she gave him a chance, she wouldn't be surprised if he tried to steal a kiss.

"You are mistaken, sir."

He seemed confused by her rebuff but shrugged it off and looked ready to strike up conversation again when more people arrived.

She was happy to disappear in the crowd as she waited for her sister's arrival.

Jane looked ethereal in a gown of silver tissue. The colour made her blue eyes pop. The king was enchanted with her. His own suit of white satin seemed to catch every ray of sunshine. Elizabeth knew that precious stones had been stitched into the fabric to produce this glittering effect.

The courtiers were all assembled by now and watched the king lead the queen onto the waiting barge.

Elizabeth found this festive atmosphere eerie. No one could have guessed he had executed his previous wife just three weeks ago.

She shook her head free of such thoughts and joined the other ladies on a barge that would follow behind the one holding the royal pair.

Schooling her features into a most serene smile, she watched with obvious pleasure the entertainment set out before them.

"Isn't this such a lovely day?" Madge said at her side.

Elizabeth nodded, clapping at some acrobats that had finished their performance.

"He planned it all himself. Or so they say."

"That was very kind of him to do so," Elizabeth said.

"He wants the past to be forgotten, but I...I can't seem to. I always imagine she will appear every time I round a corner."

Elizabeth looked to the young woman at her side. Seeing for the first time how pale she looked despite the chilly breeze and bright sunlight.

"Sometimes I dream of *her*, and she is angry with me and says she will wait for me in the next life. I am afraid I will go to hell for telling a lie so great…" Madge went on without a pause.

Elizabeth grabbed her wrist, squeezing hard to stop what she was about to say.

"Ouch." Madge pulled back, frowning.

"Careful with your words, Madge. They could land you in a dangerous place. Don't you know who you are speaking to? Have you mentioned this to anyone else?"

"No." Her voice was wavering.

"Listen to me. You did nothing wrong. You did what you were ordered to do. You cannot dwell on the past. Madge, it will be dangerous for you if you do. If I were not your friend, I would go report you. Do you understand me?"

Madge, who had always been a bit simple, seemed to comprehend the great danger she had nearly stumbled into and bit her lower lip.

"I am sorry," she whispered. "I did not mean anything…"

"I did not hear anything," Elizabeth said staunchly. "See a doctor to prescribe you a draft to help you sleep better at night."

Silently, Elizabeth hoped Madge would take the sound advice. She couldn't blame her for feeling the way she did. If she was a better person, she too would be losing sleep over the Anne Boleyn affair, but she had a cooler head on her shoulders.

She jumped in surprise when the first loud pop of the fireworks went off. Coloured sparks went whizzing through the air, to the delight of everyone watching.

"Amazing!" Madge said, having recovered now.

The firework display was followed by a gun salute that rattled Elizabeth to her bones. She held on to Madge for support. She bet that her little Harry would have loved to see this and hear the guns go off. He always liked to play at being a soldier. One day she would bring him to court, she swore to herself, and she would get to see his face light up with joy.

CHAPTER TWO

Greenwich was the king's favourite royal residence, and for good reason. The hunting park was excellent and the rooms felt airy rather than claustrophobic.

Elizabeth was to remain at court until they left on their first summer progress. Then she would go briefly to visit her children. She missed them dearly.

She was making plans for the little gifts she would buy them as she followed behind her sister as she walked with the Spanish ambassador. Jane was talking quite earnestly to him about something Elizabeth couldn't quite hear. She hoped she wasn't implicating herself into some plot with him.

She glanced around and spotted the king farther up, her brother on his left and Charles Brandon on the right. Today the king was dressed in crimson—a red rose among the green foliage. He seemed to be in a jovial, light-hearted mood, which everyone attributed to Jane.

Behind the king, trailing the party of gentlemen, was

a man in a long black coat. He stood out among the other brightly dressed men with his plain fashion. She knew him without having to see his face. This could only be Cromwell. The only man at court who didn't seem to care a fig about fashions. She had heard from Jane that he and the king had been closeted together for some hours this morning. It was this that probably put the spring in the king's step. Perhaps Cromwell had found some other monastery to tear down, pouring the riches into King Henry's coffers.

These days nothing seemed to please the king more than money.

He had made grand plans to have Jane crowned but had quickly decided to defer the ceremony for another time. Henry loved to make a great show, but with his treasury so depleted he would not be able to. It probably grated on his nerves.

They enjoyed the nice morning strolling through the garden and even listening to a lute player at the end of the pavilion.

By all accounts this would be another perfect day, but as they were heading back to the chapel to hear mass, Elizabeth watched with trepidation as her sister knelt at her husband's feet.

She immediately tensed.

Elizabeth felt the urge to rush forward and pull her to her feet. Behind the king, among the men, her brother had pushed forward. He seemed to have the same idea as her, but of course he couldn't just brazenly leap in front of her.

"Your Majesty, husband, I beg you to allow Lady Mary to come back to court as our beloved daughter," Jane said in that gentle tone of hers.

The king's eyes narrowed and his lips pursed.

"Get up."

Jane remained kneeling before him, her head bowed.

"Please, sir, I beg you to consider—"

"Stand up this instant. I will not have you embarrass me like this."

It was a command. Jane would have no choice but to do as he wished. She remained kneeling and turned a pleading gaze upon Henry, but he was impassive. Elizabeth recoiled at the displeasure on his face. She couldn't imagine what her sister must be feeling. She had to hand it to her: Jane was not showing any signs of fear.

"You do not have any favours you could ask of me now, madam. You should be on your knees thanking me for elevating you to your current station. You should be worried about the rights of our future children, not those of my bastard child. Get up. I will not ask you again."

Elizabeth felt her own mouth go dry at his words.

She was both irritated with her sister and afraid for her. What must she have been thinking? Elizabeth stole a glance at the Spanish ambassador, who looked pale and like he was wishing himself away from this land.

It should be him that faced Henry's wrath, not her sister. Unable to help herself, she scowled at him.

That afternoon, as they watched a tennis match, she felt someone slink up behind her.

"You show some solid insight and strength of character."

"Why would you say such a thing?" She didn't need to turn her head to know it was Richard Rich behind her.

"My master noticed how displeased you looked with the Spanish ambassador."

"You are mistaken. He is mistaken. I have no idea what you are talking about." Her eyes were on the court, but she couldn't deny that her breath had hitched in her throat. Her palms were growing sweaty, but she did her best to act as if nothing was amiss.

"Lord Cromwell has a message for you."

"What message could he have to give to me?"

He chuckled, and she felt a piece of paper slip into her hands.

Elizabeth grasped it but did not comment. With that, Master Rich was gone. Good riddance. She resisted all her urges to read the message until she was alone in her room that night. She hadn't spoken to Jane about what happened in the morning, but she felt sure that her brothers would have berated her soundly for her actions already.

She unfurled the note, seeing the steady scrawl of a lawyer's hand. She had no way of knowing if it really was from Cromwell himself or merely one of his many scribes.

You could be of some service to me, Lady Elizabeth. Tell me what our little Moorish friend wants, and I will see that you have a little manor house and your children back in your keeping. —C

She crumpled the note and was about to throw it into the fire, but she stopped herself. Information was power, evidence even more so. She would keep this little piece of nothing, and with that thought she tucked it away in her pocket.

Why would he even think to try to get her to spy for him? How ludicrous that he thought she would. He had struck home though, with the offer to have her children back in her keeping.

The master of spies knew everything. Even her heart's desire.

A week passed and she had said and done nothing. She didn't even show Edward the little note. Edward would probably advise her to jump on the opportunity to gain so much for so little.

But that was just the problem. It was too easy. Even with all the wealth Cromwell had at his disposal, there was no reason for him to make her such a generous offer.

The more she thought about it the more she realized how foolish she had been to even entertain the thought. Cromwell had a litany of spies at his disposal. He had spies in all the courts of Europe—he didn't need her. He was just playing a game with her. Seeing what she would do.

The king seemed to have forgotten his bad temper with Jane, and seeing as she had returned to being as docile and temperate as she had been before, he calmed as well. King Henry announced that this year they would travel all the way to York on progress.

It was on one of their little hunting trips that Elizabeth was surprised to find Cromwell move away from her brother and come toward her. A smile graced his lips.

"What a pleasant day for a hunt, is it not, Lady Ughtred?"

"It is, Lord Cromwell." She bobbed him a curtsy, more out of deference for the power he held than any actual respect for him.

"You have a beautiful horse. Your brother was just telling me that he bought it for you last year."

"She is a wonderful mare. Not afraid of anything." She couldn't look away from this intimidating man. She had the distinct impression that if she did he would strike.

"I have not received a response to my note." His words were blunt but spoken quietly so they would not be overheard. "I am not in the habit of being kept waiting."

She shifted from one foot to the other. She couldn't decide how to deal with this unreadable man. She settled on the truth.

"There was nothing for me to say."

"Have I guessed it wrong, then? You don't want to see your children again?"

"Oh, no, your arrow flew straight and true," she said in the flowery language of the court. "But I did not wish to pay the toll."

"It would cost you very little."

"Yes, exactly." She turned her sharp gaze on him. "Why would it cost so little? Unless it would be to make me indebted to you."

He couldn't hide his amusement and nodded his head to acknowledge she was right.

"What I don't understand is why you would even bother. You can pay thousands of other people to listen at keyholes or be where they aren't supposed to be. Why me?"

"I thought you might be of some use to me. I've been watching you for quite some time. I appreciate a clever mind. You aren't easily fooled or tempted, as you have proven. I might even venture to call you loyal to your family."

She couldn't stop the laugh from escaping her lips. She didn't care that she drew attention to them.

"You have a wonderful turn of phrase, Lord Cromwell. One can never be sure if they are being flattered or insulted."

"I'm glad you think so. Well, consider working with me. I think we could help each other." After a pause he added, "For both our benefit."

Elizabeth flashed him a smile. "I'll keep it in mind."

He tipped his hat to her and left.

Edward was quick to come to her side.

"What did he want with you?"

She tossed her head back, trying to seem unaffected. "Nothing. He was just bored and looking to see if he could make some trouble for himself," she said, trying to reassure him.

He looked doubtful but didn't press her further.

"I hope you were courteous at least. We need him on our good side. The king is calling a council tomorrow to have them look into the matter with Lady Mary."

Elizabeth's eyebrows rose up in surprise. "He's proceeding against her?"

Edward nodded. "I'm afraid so. But I am not lifting a finger to help her further. You saw how he reprimanded our sister."

"She should not have asked him so publicly."

"Jane thought it might convince him to listen to her."

"She doesn't know how to handle him. It's a miracle he married her at all," Elizabeth said carelessly.

"A man isn't some creature to be handled or trained."

"Isn't he?" Elizabeth grinned at him, pleased to see him defensive. "That isn't what I really meant to say. I meant that she doesn't know what he likes or how to read his moods. She's not the best judge."

"She will learn with time. There is Anne. I will go speak to her."

Elizabeth watched him run off to be at his new wife's side. She wondered how much time Jane would have to learn what the king wanted before he grew bored or displeased with her. She didn't understand how everyone could act as though Anne Boleyn had never existed.

No one had thought it would be possible for the king to be so cruel as to imprison his own daughter. No one thought the king would be willing to send his own daughter to the block. But he was inches away from doing it. Only the nervous councillors, afraid of upsetting the Emperor Charles, urged him to give Mary one more chance to recant.

Elizabeth had seen the large deputation of lords prepare to ride out to Hunsdon. Edward had not been among them. He had been spared from the unpleasant task of harassing the heiress of England into obeying her father. Thomas Howard, Duke of Norfolk, having survived the fall of his niece, was among the party. The king was exacting payment now for allowing him to retain his position at court, and he demanded results.

Arthur Darcy appeared in the queen's rooms and joined them for a game of cards. He sat beside her without her invitation and seemed eager for the chance to have a conversation with her.

She tolerated him as he divulged all he'd heard from the court gossip.

It took all of Elizabeth's power not to stare at him open-mouthed as he recalled how the Duke of Norfolk, driven to anger, threatened to bash Lady Mary's head against the wall until it was as soft as a baked apple.

"He did no such thing!" Elizabeth was aghast.

Arthur smiled. It was a thin, malicious sort of smile. Did he take pleasure in recounting such tales?

"But he did. He said that if Lady Mary did not set aside her impudent pride within the hour, he would drag her outside into the courtyard and order her head chopped off as a traitor."

Her mouth went dry. "You must be mistaken. The king would never…"

Arthur shrugged. "He was probably bluffing, but who knows what the king told him he was allowed to do. In any case, she complied."

"She signed the document?"

Darcy was happy to have her rapt attention and seemed to be eager to keep the conversation going rather than divulging everything and getting to the point right away. He kept her on the edge of her seat. She played at cards so poorly she lost fifty shillings. She'd have to borrow the money from Edward when she got the chance.

"In any case, she signed, and Parliament is making her sign another document, saying her mother and father were never truly married and that she is a bastard."

"After all this time she has finally agreed?"

"The ambassador could do nothing more for her. He told her to sign," Darcy said.

Elizabeth stole a glance at Jane. She was working on some embroidery, her face hidden by her hood. So the ambassador's gamble had failed. The Seymours had proven useless. Would they now lose the friendship of the Spanish?

"Gray suits you."

Elizabeth was startled out of her thoughts by the compliment. She looked down at her gown. It was beautifully dyed to imitate silver. Her husband had given it to her after the birth of their son. It had reminded him of the dark sea around the island they lived on.

"You are too kind," she said, her tone becoming cool once more.

Out of the corner of her eye she could see him frowning. "Have I offended you in some way?"

"It's hard to say. Are you flirting with me for boredom's sake, or do you have any honourable intentions toward me? Or perhaps you are wondering if I would be interested in another sort of arrangement? I have no interest in playing games with you. I would not risk dishonouring my name to fool around with you."

He seemed taken aback by her frankness.

"Lizzy, I have always had a soft spot for you. I meant no harm. I swear on my honour."

She nodded but turned her head away from him.

Arthur Darcy was a man who saw himself as the chivalrous knight in a sonnet. She knew she had struck a chord with him when she accused him of wanting to have a dalliance with her. But he had not said anything to the contrary. He could have declared his love for her and that he wished to marry her. He had not. She was the simple country girl he had deigned to shower his attention on. In his mind, she should be grateful. She should be fawning over him. She was good enough for a tumble underneath the sheet, but...marriage? No.

Even as the sister to the queen she was still not good enough for him. Apparently.

They played another hand at cards, and then Elizabeth excused herself.

She sat beside Jane, asking her if she needed anything.

"Shall I ask for more candles to be lit? The light in here is growing dim. You wouldn't want to harm your eyes."

Jane blinked a few times before nodding. She had been lost in thought and had not noticed how much she was straining her eyes.

Elizabeth could tell she was in a sour mood.

"You did your best," Elizabeth said, deciding she needed a kind word or two right now. "No one can fault you."

Jane shrugged. "I don't have much influence. That much is clear. I would have liked to help her more. For her sake as much as her mother's. I hope now she can come to court and all will be forgotten."

"You must look out for yourself too. You can't help everyone."

Jane threw her a look. "I will not be selfish either."

"One could never accuse you of being that. You are all sweetness, Your Grace."

She was rewarded with a little smile. "You are probably the only one telling me to look out for my own interests. If my nature would allow it, I would listen to you."

"At least you can admit your faults," Elizabeth shot back with a grin.

Jane set aside her needle and thread. One of her many attendants took it from her and tucked it away. "Perhaps I will go for a ride before dinner. Some fresh air and exercise will do us all good."

Arthur Darcy's' information had been accurate. The former princess had been forced to sign a paper declaring that she acknowledged her father was never truly married to her mother. She disinherited herself with one stroke of the pen. Lady Mary had done what was necessary for her survival. Her father had been eager to make an example of her.

Now that King Henry had announced that he had accepted Mary's apology, the Spanish ambassador seemed to breathe easier. The former princess was no longer facing the threat of the axe.

Jane, eager to begin making amends, called for her jewels to be brought to her. She picked through the extravagant pieces until she came upon a large diamond ring.

Elizabeth recognized it as one of Katherine of Aragon's jewels.

"This belongs to her. I think her mother would have wanted her to have it," Jane said, holding it up for everyone to see. The king, who had been talking to Dr. Butts nearby, looked up, frowning.

"What do you mean by that, wife?"

"Pardon?"

"Are all these jewels not my own to do what I please with?"

Jane faltered under his scrutinizing gaze. She opened her mouth to say something, but no words came out. Everyone knew that the king had not honoured the late queen's will, but only a mad person would bring this up to him.

Elizabeth, knowing Jane better than anyone else present in the room, knew she was about to say the wrong thing. Without any hesitation, she stepped forward as though to examine the ring's finery.

"You are right, sister. It is such a fine piece. Lady Mary would be reminded of the glittering court and her father, who she has not seen in many years. It shines as brightly as his majesty. Isn't that right, Jane?" Elizabeth turned to look at her.

Jane nodded, grateful for the interruption. "I misspoke earlier. I would think any daughter would be happy for a reminder of her illustrious father. May I give her this ring to remind her of you?"

The king seemed mollified for the present and, happy to appear generous, nodded in assent.

~

Thus Elizabeth found herself among the train of ladies who travelled to Hunsdon House to witness the reunion between father and daughter. Jane, nervous but excited, rode at the front of the procession beside the king. She couldn't wait to see Lady Mary again. Jane saw her as a strong ally and potential friend. She wanted her approval to sit on her mother's throne.

It was at times like these that her lack of confidence shone through. Elizabeth could not say anything to persuade her to learn to stand on her own merits.

There were a few things her sister could have learned from Anne Boleyn, and confidence was one thing.

Already Elizabeth felt the king losing interest in her sister. His eyes frequently drifted past her to other ladies in her chambers. Luckily, Jane wasn't one to make a big fuss if he bedded other women.

They rode up the stone pathway to the entrance of Hunsdon. In the large courtyard, Lady Mary waited for her father, her back straight and unyielding.

Elizabeth felt pity for her, as all eyes seemed to be examining her.

Yet Mary did not falter, and that showed some strength of character. She was small in stature, and her face was grave as she curtsied to her father and then to Jane.

Her fair hair had darkened since the last time Elizabeth had laid eyes on her. She had the seriousness of a nun. King Henry had dismounted and kissed her cheeks, pleased with what he saw as her obedience to him.

With an arm on her shoulders, he spoke to his councillors.

"Some of you here would have wished me to put this creature to death. Shame on all of you. She is my loving daughter."

At his words, Mary swayed and seemed to have fainted. Both Jane and the king rushed to her aid, and she came to moments after.

They led her inside to her privy chamber, where they might speak in private. Elizabeth saw how pale Mary had become. The king was cruel for mentioning that at all. Before the doors closed, she saw how the young girl's eyes darted around, as terrified as any colt being shoed for the first time.

Lady Mary had been taught who was truly in command, and it was a lesson she was not likely to forget any time soon.

CHAPTER THREE

As promised, Jane released her from her service for the summer. The court was to travel to Kent and make its way up as far north as Ludlow if the weather and the king's temper held.

Elizabeth was happy to pack up her things and go home to her children. She had grown tired of the pretence they all seemed to be holding up at court. But it was hard to ignore the little comments the king made when his facade would fall away and expose him for the wife killer he was.

Edward came to see her off with her little trunk and possessions loaded up in the litter.

"You really should speak to Jane to see if she could do something for you. Perhaps we should be considering who you might marry next. Now that you are sister to the queen you should have fair prospects," he said.

"I should, but for now I prefer to visit with my children and serve the family. I am not eager to jump into another marriage," Elizabeth said, tucking a stray strand of hair back in her hood.

"You are young. I cannot imagine you living out your days as a spinster nun." Edward frowned. "What life would that be?"

She smiled at him, knowing he meant to be looking out for her. "It would not be polite to marry within a year of my husband's death. I don't need people to gossip about me."

"That is true. Well, I'll keep my ears open for you." He helped her into the litter.

Jane had lent it to her in a moment of generosity. Typically, Elizabeth would have chosen to ride, but she was tired and wished to carry her things with her rather than worry about hiring a cart.

"Write to me often if you can find the time, Edward. Take care of yourself and send my regards to everyone else," she said, leaning out the opening.

He doffed his cap to her and she laughed, waving in return as the driver set off, kicking up a cloud of dust.

∼

Elizabeth had hoped to be able to rest on the journey to Yorkshire, but she found herself playing over the greeting with her children over and over again.

The wheat was growing tall in the fields, the stalks bending in the warm summer breeze.

As she passed through small towns and villages, small crowds gathered to gawk at the royal litter. Now she regretted bringing such attention to herself. Whenever they stopped for the night at an inn, she always felt like she was being taken for a fool and charged an increased price. On the other hand, she was given the best rooms and served the freshest cuts of meat and bread.

It took her over a fortnight of heavy travel to reach Yorkshire.

Her head was sticking out the window of the litter like she was a young child again, but she wanted to see the sight of the ruins of the familiar battlements as they approached. The manor house was on the site of an old Norman keep. Passing through the crumbling walls made one feel as though they were stepping back in time.

But then suddenly the steepled roof of a large manor house could be spotted peeking through the trees.

This was as fine a house as any the king owned and just as richly furnished. Its only fault was that it was too small to house a royal household, and the family too unimportant.

But what the Ughtreds lacked in prestige, they made up for in wealth.

Even Elizabeth wasn't quite sure how they had amassed so much gold. When her father had made the match, he had been uneasy about accepting the proposal from such a poorly connected family, but a tempting bribe had been too hard to resist.

Edward would never understand what it was like to be paraded like a mare at the market sold to the highest bidder. She knew that complete freedom would not be in her grasp, but at the very least she hoped she could pick her next husband.

As the litter pulled to a stop in front of the great wooden doors, they were flung open by servants. Out walked her ex-father-in-law, still standing tall after so many years in the saddle.

He kissed her hand in greeting and assured her that her children were well before she could even phrase the question.

"Come inside and rest. You must be tired after the long journey," he said with a grand courtesy he had never shown her before. But the last time she had seen him, her sister had not yet been married to the king.

Elizabeth assured him she was not weary.

"I just wish to see them," she said, hoping her tone did not sound too pleading.

He was studying the litter she had ridden in. She knew he was calculating how much the gold gilding was worth and the cost of the carpenters to carve out the intricate designs on it.

"Pardon?" He looked down at her.

She gave him her friendliest smile.

"I think I shall go say hello to the children before settling in. Are they in the nursery?"

He nodded briskly before turning his attention back to the litter.

"I'll oversee things here. Not to worry."

She looked over her shoulder and saw that her brother's secretary was overseeing the unloading of her trunks. She wouldn't have to worry.

"You are too kind." She smiled again and left before he could say anything else.

Her heart pounded as she walked the familiar halls to her children's rooms. They were still so young and close in age that they were being housed together, sharing their nurses and servants between them.

In her haste, Elizabeth threw open the door rather abruptly, even forgetting to knock.

"Milady." The nursemaid rocking her baby daughter dropped into a tiny curtsy.

In the corner, playing with a wooden ring, Henry started bawling.

"Oh, I'm so sorry." She dropped down to his level. "Mama didn't mean to scare you. Hello, Henry." She reached out for him. He seemed hesitant, his eyes traveling over to the wet nurse, who must have given him some encouragement because he stepped forward.

Unable to help herself, Elizabeth pulled him into a tight embrace.

"I missed you so much," she said, planting a kiss on his head. His dark hair was still so soft, but he had grown in the months since she had last seen him. "You will be taller than me soon," she said as she released him.

He liked the compliment and straightened up.

"Grandpère says Henry will be tall. Bigger than him."

Her lips spread in a wide grin to match his own. Surprised to see how even his speech had improved. He could barely string a few words together the last time she had seen him.

"And very strong too." She flattered his vanity.

He puffed out his chest. "Yes, I am going to have a pony."

"You are too young." Elizabeth frowned.

"No, I am not."

Seeing it wasn't a battle she was likely to win, she relented. "Fine. But I want another hug."

He flew into her arms more willingly this time, probably seeing this as a good trade.

Elizabeth stood up, rearranging her skirts just as the nursemaid was coming over to her with her little Mag. Margery had been born after her husband's death. It was amazing to imagine that in a few months she would be a year old.

She took her in her arms, admiring her plump cheeks and bright blue eyes. Those eyes reminded her of Jane's. Elizabeth couldn't be sure if Margery could actually remember her or if she was just a happy baby because she was cooing and smiling up at her with such wild abandon. It melted her heart.

"Is she eating well?" she asked the wet nurse who entered the room.

"Very well, milady. I've never seen such a sweet creature. Hardly ever cries."

Elizabeth kissed her baby's head before giving her another embrace, smelling the clean scent of linen and rose oil that was rubbed into her skin.

Her time in Yorkshire was like a dream. The sun was out every day and the weather stayed temperate. In the evenings, she would take the children out to watch the sunset and have a picnic on the lawn. When her daughter woke up during the night, she would be the one to soothe her back to sleep, sometimes resorting to taking her on walks around the manor, showing her the stars through the windowpanes.

This simple life soothed her troubled mind.

If only she had been left a good fortune to live off of. She would stay in the country forever.

Her reprieve ended when a rider dressed in her family's livery came riding up the pathway with a sealed letter addressed to her.

She put off reading it and instead tucked it away in the pockets of her gowns before sending off the messenger to get a warm meal in his belly.

After seeing her children to bed, she broke the seal and read the letter.

Sister,

I hope this letter finds you well and that you are enjoying your time with your children. Tell Henry if he behaves I will take him into my household and have him trained up to be a great warrior. I can guess what you are thinking, but you must not worry for his safety.

The reason I am writing is that the king has given me the great honour of making me Viscount Beauchamp. The ceremony will take place as soon as the court returns to London in September. Anne will have gone into confinement and I know she would wish for your company. Jane won't say anything, but I know she would benefit from seeing you as well. It is time for you to come back to us. Let me know if you need any money for the road and make sure to ride out properly guarded. We've heard whispers of disquiet in the north and I worry for your safety. I heard from Thomas that Father is unwell. Perhaps you would visit him at Wolf Hall on your way.

Writing to you from Hatfield Palace, this warm summer day,

Edward, the future Viscount Beauchamp

She couldn't help but smile imagining Edward's pride at being made a viscount in his own right. She could also picture Thomas bristling. As the middle brother, he was always jealous and wanted to prove he was superior to Edward.

Only their youngest brother, Henry, had a cool head on his shoulders. He was happiest away from court. He wanted a peaceful life, and even though he might crave wealth and prestige, he was happy with what he was given.

He would be married soon and had told Elizabeth he planned to settle with his wife near Wolf Hall. His job of administering Jane's estates would keep him away from court anyway.

"Are you to leave us soon, then?"

She was surprised by the voice behind her. She looked over her shoulder and saw her father-in-law watching her.

"Yes, I am to return back to my sister's service."

"An honourable endeavour. How are things in London? Are we to return back to Rome?"

Elizabeth frowned. "What do you mean, sir?"

He motioned for her to follow him and he led her to the garden, where they might talk undisturbed.

"The king in his wisdom reformed the church, but perhaps he went too far? Or he realizes now that he owes his obedience to the church in Rome. You and your family were always staunch Catholics. You never dabbled in heresies. It is why I chose you to marry my son. You weren't like that witch of a woman."

Elizabeth was glad for the dim light of the setting sun. She could feel her expression growing tense. He was heading toward treason, and she wasn't sure how to veer him off his course.

Did he suppose her sister would be able to change the king's mind?

"I do not know the king's pleasure, but I obey him in everything, as my sister does too."

He caught her poignant words of warning and looked down at her with a tender smile.

"I suppose it is too soon to know anything. I am sure once your sister gives the king a son he will come around."

"I pray she will give him a son as well," Elizabeth parroted back.

"Any chance of that happening soon?"

She blushed a little, unused to being interrogated by her father-in-law in this manner, but he had always been a businessman at heart.

"When I left she was not, but who knows what has happened since then. It is hard for women to tell sometimes, especially when it is their first time."

He nodded. "You didn't have any problems. If my son had lived, you would have another big belly by now. Your family was always fertile. I am sure there are no reasons to worry for your sister."

She gave him a strained smile. "There is no reason to worry."

"Right you are. But listen, I brought you here to pass you a message for your brother, or your sister, or even the king if you dare. The people are not happy in the north. They don't like these restrictions. It is a hard life and the church has always been their one place of solace. Now they are closing the monasteries and plan to close the bigger ones too. I, myself, want to obey the king in everything, but I fear how the people will react to these changes. I worry for my safety and that of your children if they were to rise up."

"And do you think they will?" she interjected, grasping her hands to keep them from shaking. "Are the children truly in danger?"

"I apologize. I should not have said anything to trouble you. I will travel south with them at the first sign of disquiet, though I would not wish to leave my lands," he said, trying to reassure her now.

They came around a bend in the path. The shrubs had grown tall here and they were hidden from sight.

"Thank you," she said, her tone uncharacteristically timid and quiet. "I would take them into my keeping if you would let me."

"Ah, not to worry yourself. I am sure your family will make another grand marriage for you and you will have new children to distract you." He patted her shoulder.

It felt as though she was being hammered back into her place.

"These are my grandchildren. Henry is my heir, and I will have him in my keeping to ensure he's raised as a man should be. When Margery is old enough, perhaps I will send her to you. Ask your brother if he will pay for her wardship." His tone carried a finality to it that she dared not argue with. "I am not doing this to be cruel. It is the way of the world, and I would never keep you from them. You may stay here as long as you choose, but you are too young to retire from the world."

Elizabeth fixed her gaze on the ground, watching a large ant skitter by on its path. She had the urge to squash it with her slippered foot. When at last she looked up, she had schooled her features into a mask of cool indifference.

"You are probably right. I get emotional over the children. They are my one joy."

He nodded. "As it goes with all proper women. How shall you get to London? Do you need an escort?"

"I shall write to my brother to provide one. I should head back inside. I am tired." She curtsied to him and turned to leave, but he called out again.

"Don't forget what I told you. Tell your brother, or even the king if you can."

She turned her head and said, "You should write to Lord Cromwell. He manages everything and he should know if there is unrest—if he doesn't already know."

She walked off, intent on getting to bed on time, but first she had a letter to write. Her brother's messenger wouldn't wait around forever.

～

Knowing she would have some time before anyone would arrive to take her back to London, she tried to spend every waking moment with her children. Margery was constantly in her arms as they chased Henry around in little games she invented for him.

Elizabeth was there encouraging Margery to take her first little steps. When she managed to toddle from the foot of her bed to her outstretched arms they celebrated by eating fresh cream with berries picked from the garden.

With each passing day the ache in her chest grew, knowing that any moment now someone would arrive to fetch her away.

So she was not surprised when one of her father-in-law's men popped his head into the nursery one afternoon to let her know she was wanted.

"Some men from London have arrived just now," he said.

"Thank you. I will come see them," Elizabeth said, tears threatening to spring from her eyes.

"Mama?" Henry asked.

She forced herself to smile. "Yes, dearest?"

"Are you sad?"

"A little," she said, deciding to be honest. "I shall miss

you very much if I have to go away."

"You don't have to go. We can play all day here and you can be the dragon and I'll be the knight," he said.

"But how will I be able to get you such lovely presents? A growing boy like you will need a real sword soon, and maybe even a horse of his own."

His eyes gleamed at that. "You can go, then, but come back very soon!"

"I will probably still be here for a day or two more. Don't worry."

He nodded. Henry still didn't understand the concept of time very well. She was sure a day or two felt like an eternity to him.

Giving Margery's cheeks a small pinch, she left to greet whoever had arrived to retrieve her.

She descended the steps, tucking the stray strands of hair back in her cap.

She was caught off guard when she spotted someone she never expected to see here, in deep discussion with her father-in-law.

Elizabeth had to grab on to the railing to keep from falling as her foot missed a step.

The noise she made alerted both men, and their eyes shot in her direction.

Arthur Darcy swept her an exaggerated bow.

It felt as though something was caught in her throat. She couldn't speak and had to fight the urge to run.

Taking a deep breath, she walked down the rest of the steps, forcing herself to keep a smile plastered on her face.

"Lord Darcy, what a surprise to see you here." She stretched out her hand to him.

He placed a chaste kiss on it.

"Your brother gave me a great honour in selecting me to come fetch you back to court. I bring messages from your family."

"Am I still to go to Wolf Hall, then?" she said, hoping against all hope that he would say no and they wouldn't have to be in each other's company for a prolonged amount of time.

"I am instructed to bring you there first. When shall you be ready to leave?"

She winced before giving a little shrug of her shoulders and looking to Lord Ughtred.

"How soon could my things be packed away? A day or so?"

"I would say two days for sure."

"Good, I will have some time to rest. It would be an honour to be shown about this beautiful house," Darcy said.

Elizabeth knew what he was hinting at, but she gave both men her most gracious smile.

"Well, I shall be ready to go in two days, then. For now I must go. I promised the children an outing. Please excuse me." She curtsied to both and retreated.

It seemed as though the sound of her heart pounding was the only thing she could hear as she went back upstairs. She must have appeared furious because no one dared speak to her as she went on her way.

How dare Edward send Darcy here? Didn't he know how much she loathed him?

By the time she calmed down she reasoned that it was quite likely he did not know. They were as close as a brother and sister could be, but even she was not comfortable discussing such things with him.

In all likelihood, Edward probably thought he was doing her some favour. Arthur Darcy seemed like a good match, but even if he was interested in marriage she could not forget how he behaved toward her and other women.

If he regarded her with any less respect or significance, she knew he would have pulled her into some hayloft and gotten what he wanted from her and been done with it. How could anyone marry someone like that? How could anyone like someone like that? Like a shield, the name "gentleman" protected any nobleman from scrutiny. Few of the noblemen actually lived up to the expectations. Then you had commoners, like Cromwell, who had proven to be as clever and refined as any nobleman. No wonder they rose so high in the king's favour.

This was a curious realization to her.

She wasn't sure anyone she knew would approve.

~

Two days was a surprisingly short amount of time left to her. Elizabeth did not bother overseeing the packing of her things. She made excuses to go somewhere with the children. She even ate her meals with them. It proved useful, seeing as she wanted to avoid Darcy as much as possible.

On the day of their departure she prided herself in keeping her eyes dry. She had shed as many tears as she could last night. It helped knowing how much Henry still remembered and seemed to love her. Margery was growing well too, and hopefully she would be able to see them again for the Christmas season.

Claiming an ache in her belly, she rode in the litter though she was perfectly capable of riding back to London.

Arthur Darcy held her hand as she climbed the steps, his hand lingering a bit too long over hers.

She hoped he would ride with the men as they set out, but he stayed by her side. Her lady-in-waiting sat across from her, and she was grateful that the seat was taken, lest Darcy get any ideas.

As she waved goodbye to the children, she saw with a sinking heart that Margery was crying for her. Her arms flailing out toward her. The nursemaid was trying to calm her down.

Elizabeth had to bite the inside of her cheek to keep from crying. They set off and she blew her children one last kiss.

"She will forget, don't worry."

"And you have much experience with children, do you?" she couldn't help but snap.

Arthur Darcy seemed taken aback by this sudden attack but tried to recover the situation.

"It is to your credit that you care so much for them and them for you. I merely meant to reassure you. I know you are emotional right now. As I know women often are."

Elizabeth was fuming. She had to squeeze her gloves in her hands to keep from saying something she would regret. After all, he was here to protect her. Why provoke him?

She did not speak for a long time but finally decided she might turn the subject away from the world she was leaving behind and his misguided ideas about women.

"Is there unrest, Lord Darcy? My brother mentioned something in his last letter to me. I have been distracted and have not been keeping abreast of the news."

He nodded, looking about him as though some ambush might descend upon them at any moment.

"There have been some minor peasant uprisings. The harvest was poor this year, and the reformations certainly sparked a fury in the simple folk. The king will show them the error of their ways."

"By force?"

He tilted his head. "Are you worried?"

"I worry for my children's safety," she said, hating that she had to explain herself. Perhaps, despite her curiosity, she should have kept quiet.

"This is nothing to worry about. If you must fear something, then fear the Spanish. They are threatening to bring the might of their empire down on us."

Elizabeth's gaze turned to the road ahead. The dirt path was well worn by constant travellers, but it was not a well-maintained road. Shrubs and other greenery were growing high on either side.

It would make it easy for any robber to ambush them right now.

She couldn't bring herself to fear some outside foreign invader when there was still so much danger close to home.

Sometimes she felt that, like this road, the kingdom was equally mismanaged, but who was she to comment on this? Could she blame the hungry peasants of the north for demanding food? Their religion nourished them both spiritually and literally. Now that the monasteries were to be torn down, who would hand out food in times of trouble?

The nobles who bought up the land certainly wouldn't.

As greedy as some of the religious houses were, none were as tight-fisted as these new landowners.

She had heard of a bill brought before Parliament that wanted to set aside money to assist the poor, but it went no further than being read by the lords, who must have balked at its contents.

Elizabeth slumped in her seat. The motion not escaping him

"You will be at court soon and all will be forgotten. If I were your brother, I would not have let you come for the summer. You've been upset."

Her first instinct was to lash out at him, but she was tired of trying to explain herself to someone like him.

Dorothea handed her a waterskin.

"Perhaps you are tired, milady."

Elizabeth nodded and was glad that Darcy seemed to take the hint as he rode on ahead.

They stopped at a roadside inn. It was a fine place but by no means luxurious. Arthur Darcy's first choice had been full, so they had ridden on.

He seemed annoyed and, by the sneer on his face, he felt that the inn was not up to his standards.

Elizabeth watched with some sympathy as the owner seemed to run about trying to please him.

She retired early, asking only that something to eat be brought to her.

"I don't mind what it is. Even a bit of bread would be fine with me," Elizabeth said, trying to reassure the innkeeper's wife.

She received a broad smile for her troubles.

As she climbed the steps up to the second floor, she could hear Darcy barking orders at his men.

How much longer would it take them to reach Wolf Hall and then London? She tried to calculate.

Her room was comfortable and the bed linen was clean. She slipped on her robe and had a cup of ale by the fire before climbing under the sheets.

She was drifting off to sleep, but an itch in her throat was bugging her. So she asked Dorothea to see if the kitchen could boil her up a quick tisane.

She nodded and left the room, promising to be back soon.

Elizabeth was so lost in her thoughts that she barely registered what she'd said. Then she heard the door handle rattling. It was faint but insistent. She froze. Was it some thief? She said a prayer in gratitude that Dorothea had the good sense to lock the door behind her.

She looked around the room. There was a poker by the fire. She looked back to the door. Would she have time to reach the poker before whoever it was broke the door down?

The door rattled again and she leapt out of bed, making a beeline for the poker. She would face whatever came head-on.

The next moment there were voices. She could make out Dorothea's voice, growing ever louder by the minute. The other voice belonged to a man. Another voice joined the throng. Then there was the sound of footsteps before silence.

A key was slipped into the lock. With a sigh of relief Elizabeth saw it was Dorothea who stepped through the doorway, locking it again behind her.

"Lady Ughtred!" She stepped back in shock, seeing Elizabeth standing by the fire with a poker in hand.

Elizabeth, looking sheepish now, set it down, but her heart was still pounding in her chest.

"I apologize. I was worried...what has happened?"

Dorothea looked pale.

"I found Lord Darcy trying your door."

"What?!" Even this shocked Elizabeth. She had known he was a cad, but to go so far?

"When I questioned him about what he was doing here, he said he merely wanted to talk to you and told me to be on my way. He was upset when he heard I was staying with you. Another patron heard and came to see what was the matter. His lordship made some other excuse and fled. I hope I did nothing wrong?"

Elizabeth bit her lip and closed her eyes, unable to comprehend what she was saying...and, worse, what she was implying.

"You have saved me. Of course you did nothing wrong," she said. "He was sent to guard me, but it seems that more than any other vagabond it is him I should fear the most. I don't believe his intention toward me was pure. Or at the very least I can't take that chance."

Dorothea nodded. As a woman herself she knew what it was like.

"Will you tell your brother? You could even go to the king."

Elizabeth contemplated that for a moment but shook her head.

"Any stain on our reputation is the last thing any of us would want right now. It's not worth it, and nothing happened. If he came in here, I would have stuck him with the poker."

Dorothea laughed behind her hand.

"I believe you would, milady."

It was hard for her to climb back into bed and relax,

but she tried to be calm for Dorothea's sake. She wished she didn't have to go back to court.

Eventually, exhaustion overcame her worry and she slipped into that black nothingness.

∽

The red brick walls of Hampton Court seemed to sparkle in the brilliant morning light. It was dew frosted over that caused the sparkle.

Elizabeth was riding on her horse now, wrapped in two heavy cloaks against the frosty air.

She had awoken early, and they set off at her request.

"My sister would wish me to make all haste," she had said with a false smile to Darcy. He had been sheepish around her and avoided her ever since that night.

For her part, this was exactly what she was hoping for. Her gratitude toward his shift in behaviour made her behave almost nicely to him. They both knew that she now held the upper hand. He did not know what she might do with the knowledge that he had tried to barge into her rooms.

They weren't on the road anymore. She had protectors here, credible witnesses.

The chill was uncharacteristic for this time of year, and she would be glad to get inside in a timely fashion.

The moment she dismounted her horse she went to find her brother. She did not even bother to say farewell to Arthur.

Elizabeth was admitted to her brother's chambers

and was greeted with the sight of Edward enjoying breakfast by the fire with Anne. Her belly looked so big now that even Elizabeth would suspect her of carrying twins.

She curtsied as any respectable country lady would but greeted Edward coldly. He had stood to embrace her, but she pulled away.

"What is the matter?" he said.

She arched an eyebrow at him. "What do you think? Next time, know that any of your knights, or secretaries, or chancellors, or even a squire would suffice in fetching me away."

Edward seemed taken aback to the point he took a step away from her.

"Has something...happened? I did not know you disliked him so much."

"I never liked him. He's insufferable. Being on the road with him was worse than being stricken down by the sweating sickness."

"Bless you," he said, laughing. "I thought a summer with your children would have brought you back to us as sweet as a lamb, but I see your tongue is as sharp as ever."

"Edward, you know what Darcy is like. He is so self-important and always turned his nose up at us..." She paused, taking a breath. "I suppose it doesn't matter now. It's in the past. But please, Darcy is the last person I want to have escorting me. Send me Cromwell instead."

"Heaven forbid," Anne gasped out in between mouthfuls of sausage.

"I mean it."

"Calm down, sister. I swear to you that you shall never be forced to endure his presence under my watch."

She eyed him to see if he was being sarcastic but found only sincerity. "Very well."

Then she remembered the other reason she had rushed in here.

"I saw Father, as you asked me to. He is doing poorly. He's become so thin I could barely recognize him," she began. Predictably, Edward tensed. To say he had a difficult relationship with their father would be an understatement, but he still had his duty to him. "I would have stayed by his side, but he sent me on my way. Wouldn't hear of me staying another night. Maybe…you could go see him?"

Edward shook his head. "I am needed here. But I'll send Thomas or Henry."

"If that is what you think is best."

Anne couldn't help but interject. "They can see to his funeral arrangements as well as Edward. He need not go."

Elizabeth felt as though the blood drained from her face. She hated talk of death, and to hear her father's being talked about so coldly was off-putting.

"And Jane? How is she?" she said, trying to find some way to switch the topic.

"Well," Edward said.

"How well?" Elizabeth couldn't help but press.

He merely shrugged and she took this to mean that Jane had not conceived yet.

"It's still early."

"Tell that to him," Anne said, chiming in.

Elizabeth bit back a smile. "Well, I shall go pay my respects to her."

"And I am to go to the archery butts with the king this morning," Edward said, with a bow to the pair of them.

˜

Jane's rooms were empty. A few maids remained to tidy around the room. They had to be kept meticulously clean. One could never know when the king might arrive with a foreign ambassador on his heels. Every little detail would be sure to get repeated. Soon the Venetian bankers would be talking about dirty bedsheets left lying around the royal apartments or the crumbs of food scattered on the floor. Leading a public life was not as glamorous as it would seem. Every word, deed, and breath you took was remarked upon.

Elizabeth discovered from a passing lady-in-waiting that Jane had gone to play bowls on the green. It was not a pastime she enjoyed herself, and she decided she would wait for her here.

It was after she was gone that she stopped to wonder what Margaret Douglas was doing inside on a day like today.

Lady Douglas was the king's niece and loved the importance it gave her. She loved being at the forefront of any social event. The fact that she was young, pretty, and very close to the throne made sure she was never without attention.

Elizabeth recalled her holding some folded parchment in her hand.

She couldn't imagine Margaret being a studious type of woman.

And if she wasn't studying or reading her scriptures, then what was left? A love letter? This could only spell trouble. She would mention it to Jane.

Her sister was always going with the flow, forgetting that she was supposed to be managing it. After all, she was in charge of the well-being of the ladies in her service.

She was greeted by everyone in her sister's retinue with warm interest. They were full of stories to tell. The court had not travelled far this summer, but there had been plenty of activity.

Jane greeted her with a smile and embrace after Elizabeth had curtsied to her.

She was grateful the tension between them had seemed to ease.

"How is young Henry? Has he grown much?"

Elizabeth smiled, recalling how rambunctious he had become. "Soon you won't be able to even recognize him. He won't stop chattering."

Jane had a wistful smile on her face. Elizabeth didn't have to ask what she was thinking about. Her sister was wishing for a child of her own.

Reaching over, she gave her sister's hand a light squeeze. Trying to be reassuring.

Jane pulled her hand away, her gaze moving away from Elizabeth to Jane Rochford watching nearby.

"Lady Rochford, I am pleased to see you have returned to court after such a long reprieve."

Elizabeth watched Lady Rochford sink into an exaggerated deep curtsy.

"I am so grateful to have been allowed to return. The country is no place for me."

"Even hell would have no place for you," Elizabeth said under her breath.

The flicker of a smile crossed her sister's face for the briefest of moments.

The ever-watchful Jane Rochford had not missed the exchange.

Elizabeth chose that moment to retreat, not wishing to end up in a full confrontation with yet another of her sister's ladies. She had been living on her own for far too long. The longer she was at court, the more she felt she didn't fit in. She had little patience to develop that finesse the other ladies had of cutting each other down with a look. Elizabeth had enjoyed being the lady of the manor out in the country. Her temperament was more suited for haggling with merchants than politicking at court.

She retreated to a seat by the window just as a gentleman usher announced the king's messenger.

She focused her attention on the darkening sky. Clouds were gathering on the horizon and heading this way. There would be no outing on the river tonight.

Rain was a welcome sight though. The summer had been unnaturally dry and the harvest would be doomed to be poor. And hunger fed rebellion.

CHAPTER FOUR

Several days passed, none any different from the last.
She watched her brother kneel before the king as the velvet mantle of estate was placed over his shoulders. Elizabeth wasn't listening to the herald reading out the letters patent. Her eyes watched her brother as his transformation from mere knight to baron took place.

His demeanour changed. He seemed to have grown taller and more firm on his own two feet. The shadow of their father no longer hung over him. He had lands and titles in his own right and did not have to feel beholden to his father.

Elizabeth understood how Edward had felt shackled by their father. The scandal that had nearly destroyed their family was still as fresh in his mind as it was six years ago. Edward had to pretend all was well these many years while his first wife was quietly locked away and his sons or half-brothers were disinherited.

Elizabeth had been barely out of the schoolroom at

the time. She did not know why suddenly her nephews were banished from Wolf Hall, why her father locked himself in his study, and why Edward's wife was hidden away in a convent far away.

Well...it did not take her long to piece it all together. She had been shocked to think that someone as young and pretty as her sister-in-law would be capable of batting her lashes at her old decrepit father.

To this day, Edward saw him only when absolutely necessary, and he had never brought Anne Stanhope, his new wife, to visit Wolf Hall.

It was no secret he was eagerly waiting for their father to pass on.

For her part, Elizabeth resented him for his mishandling of the situation. If her father was such a lecherous old man, could he not have been smarter about it? Could he not have picked any other lady to chase after?

Then, when it was time for her own marriage, he had not bothered to look very far or hard for a suitable husband. Thinking of his debts, he selected the older Ughtred for her to marry, seeming not to care about her happiness. The thought sickened her, but at least Ughtred had proved to be a serious godly sort of husband who had been grateful for her and kind.

"May I interrupt you?"

She was brought out of her thoughts by the question.

"Pardon?" She turned around to see who spoke. The man before her was fair, with a kindly appearance. It took her a moment to recall that this was the son of Thomas Cromwell. Like her, he had been rarely at court. Seeing him this close, she saw he bore little similarity to his father, except perhaps those dark eyes of his.

She forced herself to smile in an effort to be courteous, but it was hard to disguise the fact that she was uneasy.

"I apologize for interrupting you," he said with a tilt of his head as though he was examining her. "I was curious..." He stopped, as though he had not wanted to say that.

So he wasn't a consummate politician like his father... at least not yet. She felt reassured by this, at least somewhat.

"Was there something else, Lord Cromwell?" Elizabeth said with an arched eyebrow, waiting for him to continue.

He cleared his throat with a sheepish grin on his face. "What I meant to say is I was curious to know where you had disappeared to all summer. I would have thought you would have travelled with the court."

"Ah. That is easy enough to answer. I went to Yorkshire to be with my children. Time passed by too quickly, I am afraid."

"It is a shame they cannot just be here at court with you. Surely your family has enough room by now."

She nodded. "I am sure they would have loved to be here at court, but it is no place for them. Not yet anyway. They are so young. Although my eldest keeps insisting I bring him." Elizabeth wasn't sure why she was being so open with him. Perhaps it was the air of ease he radiated that made her relax.

"I remember begging my father to bring me to court too. It didn't help that he would return with fantastical stories of birds flying out of pies and dragons that breathed fire on the Thames. As a child, I thought the court was the happiest place of all."

"And now that you've been to court, what do you think?"

He chuckled, knowing he had trapped himself. There was only one correct, diplomatic answer. She waited to see what he would say.

"I've grown up to know that there are no dragons. But the court is even more splendid than I could have imagined."

"Well put." Elizabeth's mask of indifference cracked into amusement. Then she paused to consider him. "And will you tell me how I have managed to catch your attention?"

His sheepish grin returned.

"I was told it would be worth my time getting to know you. My father says you are an interesting woman, and he never compliments anyone lightly."

"I see. I suppose I shall be honoured, then." Her eyes drifted away from his face to his hands that were fidgeting with the purse strings at his belt.

"I..."

She looked back up at him. "There's no need to be embarrassed."

He shook his head and shifted from one foot to the other. "Now I have the desire to turn back time. Words do not come so easily to me as they do for my father. I always seem to say the wrong thing."

"Then we have that in common."

He adjusted his cap, the ruby pin in it catching the light.

It was the first time she'd noticed it. His clothes were cut in the latest fashions, but he had not overdone it. Instead, he appeared stylish rather than ostentatious in his display of wealth. She appreciated that in a man. It was so easy to look foolish decked from head to toe in jewels and expensive cloth.

"I shall add generosity and kindness to the list of your many virtues."

Feeling coquettish, she batted her eyes. "How very kind of you. What else is on that list, I wonder?"

Now she watched his eyes flash with mischief. "I would hate to be such an open book."

"Very well." Elizabeth was feeling slightly disappointed.

A blare of trumpets announced that the feast was starting.

He offered her his arm and she gladly took it. Elizabeth was surprised to find that her initial distrust of him had dissipated.

The banquet hall was decorated with garlands and elaborate displays of flowers. Blooming red and white roses created a huge Tudor rose that took up the whole of the back wall.

"How beautiful," she couldn't help commenting.

Many people were streaming in, staring with equal wonder at what the master of ceremonies had concocted.

"My father has outdone himself this time," Gregory said, looking toward the huge rose.

"He ordered this?"

His lips twitched. He had spoken without meaning to yet again. "Not exactly. He suggested that something to honour the Tudors would be appropriate. Something pompous. The French ambassador has been spreading rumours we are broke and the Spanish that our people are discontent."

"Is it not true what the Spanish ambassador says?" Elizabeth couldn't help but ask. "This is not the first time I have heard of such reports."

He waved his free hand. "It will be taken care of. One way or another. But the important thing is we would rather that news of our troubles doesn't travel around Europe. We cannot afford any weakness now."

"Spoken like a true politician. You explain yourself well," she said.

"And too openly."

His dark eyes met her blue ones, and she thought she saw a spark of something in them.

They had reached the table designated for the ladies-in-waiting.

"They will gossip, I am afraid. Will you be able to weather the storm?" she said with a flippant look around at the sidelong gazes she was receiving.

"I daresay I shall find the strength somewhere, and if all else fails I'll pay them to shut their mouths." He brought her hand to his lips, placing the briefest of kisses on her hand. "It was a pleasure meeting you."

"And you as well, Lord Cromwell." She gave him a little curtsy before taking her seat.

She had to force herself not to look as he walked away. Later, as the feast began and she grew bored of the dish after dish served, she fought the urge to seek him out.

She had not been mistaken in fearing the gossip-mongers.

Luckily, she had not given them much fodder and they would grow bored, but somewhere in some little book it would be written that she had let Cromwell escort her into dinner.

Acrobats and the court fool performed, to everyone's delight, all sorts of mockeries and games. The spirits of the assembly were light and the king seemed pleased with everyone. He danced only one jig before claiming he wished to sit with his beautiful bride.

Elizabeth wondered at everyone's acceptance of this lie. She worried that if he was incapable of dancing, was he also incapable of giving her sister a child? Would he not blame her?

She watched how he seemed to fawn over Jane, but Elizabeth still did not forget how he had evoked the memory of Anne Boleyn when he told her to keep her mouth shut.

Edward was too pleased with himself to do much else but preen and walk about the room, accepting the congratulations of everyone.

He stopped by her seat to greet her with a kiss.

"I am happy to see you are in better spirits now than the last time we spoke."

"Nonsense. My grievances with you have been tucked away until later. For now I want you to enjoy your victory."

"How kind. You would make a vicious enemy."

"Be glad, then, that I was born your sister. Has Thomas returned? I did not see him today," she said, looking over his shoulder. "I would have thought he would have been happy to take part in the celebrations today."

"You know Thomas," he said with a grimace. "He cannot be happy for others. He's always coveted what I was given. But it is a shame he is not here. The king decided he will make Thomas a gentleman of the privy chamber."

"He will be pleased, but he won't take it kindly to be second best to you. You are right. He will complain that he should have been made a viscount as well."

"In time he might, especially if our dear sister can please the king."

Elizabeth bit back a word of criticism. It was not Edward's place to put such pressure on Jane. She was under enough strain as it was.

"Leave poor Jane alone. She will do better without everyone watching her all the time and making comments behind her back. She pretends like she doesn't hear, but she does and she takes them to heart."

"Noted."

Elizabeth saw her brother get distracted by someone else across the room and urged him to go with a reassuring smile.

Who had time for a sister when there was power and money to be had out in the world?

"Your brother is very lucky," Lady Rochford said, taking an empty seat beside her.

Elizabeth tried her best to keep her distaste for the woman from her face. She merely inclined her head in agreement.

"My husband was given great titles when Anne married the king too. He should remember it does not always lead to happiness."

Was that a threat? Her breath got caught in her throat, despite her best efforts to remain calm.

"It is a good thing my brother has always acted in the king's best interest and has a spotless record."

Lady Rochford's laugh was a shrill sound that grated on her ears and made her wince.

"Spotless? I suppose blameless would be a better choice of words. Do you think any of us have forgotten about that business with his previous wife and your father? Is that why he keeps his new one so close? He wants to make sure this son is truly his?"

Elizabeth would have slapped her if she were not in public. She dared not create such a scene, in front of the king no less. How could Jane Rochford, of all people, dare?

She seemed to read her mind, for she grinned as she

reached over Elizabeth, plucking the wine goblet from the table, taking a swig of the blood-red liquid inside.

"I have friends. Perhaps more than even you and your lot," she said. "But do not fear. I am here as a friend."

"For now at least. Am I correct in assuming this is what you mean?"

"Shrewd as ever, Lady Ughtred."

Elizabeth wished for some dancing to begin. Then she could have an excuse to leave her seat.

"You would do well to cling to that Cromwell boy if you can. The king is pleased with his father. Perhaps he wouldn't mind being connected by marriage to him as well."

"You are nothing but vile tonight," Elizabeth said, taking the wine goblet from her hands.

"Perhaps." Jane tilted her head to the side, considering and looking forlorn as the goblet was placed out of reach.

A motion at the back of the hall caught Elizabeth's attention. The golden fabric was unmistakable as it swished away around the corner. Margaret Douglas leaving a feast early?

Jane's eyes had followed her gaze.

"Yes, that one is in for some trouble."

"Is she? Why don't you report on her, then?" Elizabeth asked.

"Who says I haven't already?"

"It would be treason not to let the king know if something untoward is happening with his niece."

Jane flashed her a toothy smile. "I know nothing. I said nothing."

"Yet you seem to have lots of information."

"Yes, it is what makes me useful. What makes you useful? Your pretty face? Your fertility?"

Elizabeth blanched at her crudeness. Jane Rochford was drunk. The smell coming from her breath and her words made the conclusion unmistakable.

"You should go to bed."

There was that shrill laugh again. "I am not some ninny you can send off to bed."

"I would have you whipped if you were," Elizabeth said under her breath. Hating that she couldn't see a way to escape this woman's company.

"I thought we were friends. Or that we could become friends. After all, aren't we both widows?"

"Not of the same calibre. I did not drive my husband to the headsman with my words. Shall you ever repent of this sin?"

"I do what I need to do to survive," Lady Rochford said, but Elizabeth could see her hands had begun to shake.

"Yes, and if you want to continue doing so, get away from me and go to bed if you have any sense."

Elizabeth stood and left, seeing her brother's wife approaching.

"Are you well? You seem pale," Anne said, looking her over.

"I am surprised Lady Rochford was ever allowed to return to court," Elizabeth said under her breath.

"Oh, no one wanted her. Least of all Jane, but Lord Cromwell commanded it."

Elizabeth raised an eyebrow at that. "So she's his spy? Well, she won't find anything on Jane."

"I am sure she won't. But there are other fish to fry, so to speak. The Duke of Norfolk also requested she join the queen's rooms, so I would not be surprised if she has two benefactors."

Elizabeth shook her head. "How does she sleep at night?"

"Probably counts her coins until she becomes exhausted."

They were joined by Mary Norris. "Is Lady Rochford well? She is behaving rather strangely."

Elizabeth was about to say the truth but felt it would not be a good move to further antagonize her.

"She is a bit under the weather. Perhaps you could help her to bed."

"I shall," Lady Norris said with a nod to the pair of them.

After she was out of earshot, Elizabeth pulled Anne to the side.

"Have you heard anyone say anything about Margaret Douglas?"

Anne looked thoughtful for a moment, placing a hand on her growing belly. "No, but to be truthful I have only been thinking of my confinement. I do not wish to go in, but I am also tired of lumbering around court like some fat cow."

"You are serious?"

"Yes." Anne furrowed her brows. "Is there anything to be worried about?"

"It's just she's been acting strange..."

"Oh, Maggie is just being young and in love," a giggling Lady Howard said nearby.

Elizabeth craned her neck to see who it was. Lady Mary Howard, daughter of Thomas Howard, Duke of Norfolk. Widow of the king's bastard son.

She had been less interested in the festivities than she had appeared to be.

Inwardly, Elizabeth wondered if there was any place at court one could go without being overheard.

"What do you mean in love?" She pinpointed that immediately.

Mary Howard threw her head back. "Not everyone is wasting their youth." But then she seemed to stop and reconsider what she was hinting at. "Nothing is happening or happened. It's just a bit of fun."

Elizabeth decided to play the part of the fool and nodded.

"Very well, I was just curious. I have noticed her disappearing a lot lately and she always seems to turn up in unexpected places." That said, she turned to Anne to inquire more about the baby and talk about her own children until she felt certain that Lady Mary had lost all interest.

Finally, she pulled Anne away. "What do you think we should do?"

"I will tell Edward. This might be important, and if

the Howards are up to something again or involved in a plot, then we should be the ones to expose them."

"Anne, how will you ever rest for a whole month in bed?"

Anne laughed. "I daresay I shall suffer."

Elizabeth gave her hand a light, reassuring squeeze. "I will pray for you and your child."

"Will you keep me company?"

"Of course, it is really why Edward sent for me. I think after my two children I have become a good luck charm. Besides, Jane is surrounded by plenty of ladies to serve her. She won't even miss me," Elizabeth said.

"Not when you consider who is around her. Taking that into account, I wouldn't be surprised if she finds you are among the best of the bunch," Anne said.

"The king's daughter will be coming to court soon, won't she?"

"There have been discussions, but nothing has been planned yet. I suppose the king has not forgiven her so quickly."

"I suppose you are right. She was lucky she saw the error of her ways so quickly."

"Ah, there is one thing you will not have heard. The Countess of Salisbury will be attending court. She has been invited once more. It is a good sign. At least I think so," Anne said, looking to her to comment.

They began walking around the room, making sure to keep their skirts away from the people passing by carrying jugs of ale or wine.

"I hope it is a good sign for Lady Mary. I don't know

what my sister has said to the Spanish ambassador, but I hope he will be satisfied and report good things to the emperor."

"You still fear that they would declare war on us?"

Elizabeth bit her lower lip. "The unrest up north cannot be caused by nothing. I think someone is fanning the smoke of rebellion, and I wouldn't be surprised if the Spanish were behind it."

"There are many who would love to see England fall. The French included."

Elizabeth shrugged. "Who am I to judge? The timing seems all too convenient. Even the Scots across the border would enjoy this opportunity."

"They are heretics as much as we are. The protestant factions are growing stronger than ever," Anne pointed out.

Elizabeth nodded her head in agreement.

Just then Edward came up to them, his cheeks red and glowing. Elizabeth wondered if it was from the drink in his hands or his pride in himself.

"What are you two lovely ladies talking about?"

"The finer points of needlework, milord," Elizabeth said with exaggerated deference.

At her side, Anne chuckled but agreed.

"Good, good," Edward was saying but then caught their mischievous looks. "I think you are lying, Lady Ughtred."

Elizabeth bit back a smile, shaking her head. "Prove it."

"I shall have to set a spy about you. I thought that you

would be here to watch over my darling wife and not set a bad example for her."

"She has done nothing of the sort, husband." Anne patted his arm, sneaking the drink out of his hand before handing it to Elizabeth. "Shall you escort me back to our rooms? I am tired."

"Very well." He placed a kiss on her mouth and led her away.

Elizabeth found herself alone, holding Edward's discarded cup. She looked at the dark red liquid swirling inside and with a shrug, drank the rest of its contents.

It was heavier than the usual variety she drank, but the taste was fruity and sweet.

She pondered her conversation with Anne. Hoping that they were both wrong and that England could enjoy years of peace without being dragged into some conflict. War was not a pleasant thing. Especially for women, who could do little else but stitch banners and pray for the safe return of their menfolk.

She joined a group of fellow ladies-in-waiting, preferring to lose herself in their banal conversation rather than focus on the serious topic everyone had on their mind but was too scared to voice.

⁓

Anne Stanhope went into confinement with her head held high. She had grown so big that she welcomed her chance to hide away from prying eyes. Everyone scared her with stories of twins or large babies that tore their mothers in half.

"Never fear," Elizabeth had told her. "What will be will be. But I have found that optimism is the best medicine. A happy mother will lead to a happy baby."

"Yes, but did you grow as big as a house?" Anne asked, a hand stroking her belly. "I cannot remember what my feet look like. I can barely walk straight without toppling over."

"It will get better. You will miss it, despite all the discomfort."

"I find that hard to believe," Anne sniffed.

Elizabeth shrugged. "You don't need to believe me. So what will you do to occupy your time?"

"Sew, embroider...send you out to collect gossip for me."

"I can do that." Elizabeth was more than happy to be given permission to leave the dark room. It wasn't that she minded so much, but she would rather be of some help rather than sitting around twiddling her thumbs. She kept thinking of her children and wrote a long letter to be sent to Yorkshire as soon as possible along with the wood carving of a horse for Henry, promising that she would send him a real one soon enough.

The first week she spent reassuring Anne all her worries were unfounded. She tried to settle her sister-in-law into a sense of security and calmness. For all her words, Anne did not handle being locked up very well and spent most of her time arguing with the priest about the necessity of it.

"I have not read anywhere in the Bible that women should be locked up in dark rooms before the birth of their children."

"Lady Seymour, it is to ensure your safety," the priest said, the shock evident in his voice.

"Anne, you should be grateful for this added security and protection," Elizabeth added.

Anne shot her a look that told her she was betraying her.

"Shall I say the final blessing?"

"Yes," Anne said, grumbling a few unheard words.

After he had left, Elizabeth looked at her with amusement. "What happened to being excited to hide away from the world?"

Anne waved her off.

"I was trying to trick myself."

"Why don't I go to Jane's rooms and see what is happening. I am sure Edward will send you a trinket today too."

"I am sure he's forgotten all about me," Anne said with a dramatic cry before sinking down onto a cushion.

"You amuse me. Anything else you would like while I am gone?"

"Can you check on Marsel? Make sure he is happy. I am sure the servants are neglecting him."

"I shall do that," Elizabeth said, though she hated saying yes. The monkey was quite...a handful. She wouldn't be surprised if the servants had let some accident befall him or turned him into a cleaning rag.

It took a moment for Elizabeth's eyes to adjust to the

full light of the day outside. Anne's rooms were kept dark and only the smallest of windows was left cracked open.

"Have you been set free?"

Elizabeth blinked. Some might call it happenstance that Gregory Cromwell had been walking by, a folder of papers in his hands.

He saw her looking at them and smiled.

"Today I am playing the errand boy for my father."

"I am playing the messenger for my sister-in-law. How amusing that our paths have crossed."

"Happenstance."

She gave him a coy smile and then with a little bow said farewell and headed on her way.

Jane's rooms were packed full of visitors today.

The Countess of Salisbury had arrived with her entourage of ladies and servants.

Elizabeth could see she was doing her best to show deference to the new queen. But Lady Margaret Pole was a woman who held much political power and experience. She had been at court during the reign of King Henry VII, witnessed the young prince Henry take up his throne and marry his first wife, Katherine of Aragon. She had been there for it all.

It was hard to pretend that she did not matter.

Back when Katherine of Aragon was queen, Jane Seymour had the privilege of darning her socks and stitching little Ks in her prayer book. Could she so easily forget this?

Elizabeth had to hand it to her though. She was a good actress. She pretended not to notice how the ladies seemed to gravitate toward her. How they cast her admiring looks. She was the envy of all but the silliest of them, who did not understand that before them was a great woman who held titles and lands in her own name. They saw her as old and spent, but in fact she was a rarity. A woman of power, with her own lands, an army of tenants she could raise, the power to buy and sell land as she pleased. No one but the king could command her.

At last Elizabeth's presence was noticed by Jane, who bid her to come over and introduced her to Lady Salisbury.

"I am glad to see you back at court, countess," Elizabeth said with measured courtesy. She tried to observe all the rules of decorum more carefully around people like her.

"I am glad to be here," Lady Salisbury said with a detached tone. "There is no place grander, or more welcoming."

Elizabeth agreed.

"I was just telling the queen how lovely it will be to have children at court again. How is Lady Seymour doing? I hear she is in her last weeks of confinement."

"You are well informed, my lady," Elizabeth said, looking over to Jane, who had maintained her composure and kept up her appearance of blank indifference.

Only a sister could have known the deep sadness and failure Jane was feeling at this moment.

"Lady Seymour is doing well. I have come to report to my sister this fact. Also that Anne has sent her love and greetings. She misses you all and cannot wait to re-join you."

"We pray she will," Lady Salisbury said with much seriousness.

Despite her serious appearance, she was well known for being a caring mistress to those around her. She reserved her hatred for those she saw as heretics.

"Please let my sister-in-law know we are thinking of her. The king and I."

Elizabeth took a seat at her sister's feet. "I shall be happy to let her know. I am sure she will be flattered."

She spent a whole hour in her sister's company before retreating to the king's side of the rooms, where her brother lingered. He was part of the privy chamber, but he was not yet one of the favourite few. That honour seemed to continue to elude him.

You wouldn't know it from looking at him. Edward had the knack of giving off an air of self-assurance. Even an ounce of that given to Jane would have improved her spirits.

"Elizabeth! Is everything well?"

She hurried to reassure him, realizing her expression had been sour.

"Anne has been missing you. She is expecting a gift. So don't forget to send her something."

"She is?" He seemed a bit puzzled.

"Well, I do remember you promising her a gift for every day she was locked away," Elizabeth said.

He grimaced. "I may have let my emotions get the best of me."

"It doesn't have to be big. Even a flower to show her you are thinking of her," Elizabeth suggested.

He thought for a moment, then plucked a ring off his finger and handed it to her.

"Tell her this is for her, my dearest love."

Elizabeth arched her brow. "Really? You think she has lost her wits too? She will know you had this lying around."

"It is new. I won it off Thomas Wyatt this morning, in a game of bowls."

"Hmm...very well. I don't want this to cause any trouble..."

"And it won't, dearest sister. It won't," he said with his usual tender care. "How does she really?"

"Anne is restless. As women tend to be during these times. It will end eventually."

"And do you think it'll be a boy this time?" Edward said.

"You already have two boys, or you would have if you hadn't disowned them."

He glared at her.

"What?"

"I would rather you not bring up that unfortunate business."

She glowered at him, refusing to give way. "I am merely speaking the truth. I cannot tell what Anne is carrying. Would you be very disappointed if it was a girl?"

"No, I think I would prefer it. The king would take it better," Edward said, scratching an itch on the back of his head. "He's been in a bad mood this month. I think our sister is still not yet with child. Should a doctor see her?"

Elizabeth shook her head. "Do you want to be accused of witchcraft?"

"A doctor could bring on no suspicion."

"Of course it could. A witch is one step away from a doctor. It makes us look desperate. It would be easy for people to believe that we were foolish enough to dabble in the dark arts."

"You think of everything, don't you? Still, I can't help…"

"Don't even say it. Don't cast doubt on it now. Jane needs us."

"You were never her strongest defender. Why the sudden change?"

Elizabeth shrugged. "I was angry. I still am, but not at her."

A man passed by and cast a sideway glance at them.

She remembered that they were not in Edward's private rooms.

"I shall go back to your wife with your gift to her."

"Send her all my love. Anything she desires shall be hers."

"Unfortunately, what she desires is exactly what you cannot give her." Elizabeth gave him a smile and waved to him as she departed.

Anne was excited to see the ring.

"It is such a fine emerald. It catches the candlelight so beautifully," she said, exclaiming over it.

One of her ladies couldn't hold herself back from

commenting, "Too bad your ladyship can only wear it on your pinkie finger."

Anne's glare was frightful and the lady backed off, apologetic.

"Don't worry about it. It is common in pregnancy. Once the baby is born you will recover."

This sent Anne wailing.

Elizabeth was unsure what to do but wrapped her arms around the sobbing woman as best as she could. "There, there. Worst case, you make Edward have all your jewellery remade or buy you new pieces."

The sobs slowed as she seemed to consider this.

"I would deserve it for all the trouble he puts me through," Anne sniffed.

"I will make sure to tell him so." Elizabeth ran a hand over her head.

At last Anne's spirits returned, and she was able to sit by the window to catch a few remaining moments of sunlight.

∾

In the end, little Edward was born two weeks late, past the date estimated by the physicians. It had been an exercise in patience for Elizabeth as much as it had been for Anne.

Luckily, the birth had been an easy straightforward one, given that Anne was a first-time mother.

The father had rushed in the very next hour to see his wife and new legitimate son. With a kiss on his forehead, he sped away before the midwives could scold him too much.

Despite what Edward had said, he was immensely proud of his new baby boy and did not mind that the king had barely said a word to him upon hearing the news.

Elizabeth tried to stay by Jane's side as much as possible, reassuring her with her silent presence. It was not long after Anne had come out of her confinement, with a triumphant glow about her, that Lincolnshire exploded into rebellion.

If she had not taken to sleeping at the bottom of Jane's bed on the small truckle bed, she might have been the last to know. Unexpectedly, one night the king charged in, a look of worry on his face as he took in his new bride, still half asleep.

"Get up. Have you not heard?" he said, pacing her room.

Elizabeth threw a robe over herself and grabbed another for her sister, who was rubbing the sleep out of her eyes.

"What is it, my lord?" Jane said in that quiet way of hers. Ready to be told what to do, what to think.

This was the right thing to do. The king was inspired to look at her like the sweet innocent maid he had married a few months ago.

"Ah, sweetest Jane. I forget myself. You would not have heard. How could you have? You don't have all sorts of visitors traipsing into your rooms in the middle of the night."

Elizabeth bit the inside of her cheek to remind

herself not to say anything. The longer she was in the king's presence, the less in awe she was of him. Had he seriously come into the queen's room forgetting who was in it? Perhaps he was half asleep himself.

"Please, tell me, my lord, how may I help you? What has happened?"

"I am furious by the reports of another rebellion in the north. I received word that just as we had finished squashing the Lincoln rebels, Yorkshire has taken up arms and is inspiring many others to do the same. They seek to tell me how to rule well. I shall teach them who is master here."

Elizabeth's heart caught in her throat. Her worst fears were coming true. Where were her children? What if they were stuck on opposite sides of this conflict? What if they were in danger?

Jane looked to her now pale face and then back at the king, unsure of what to say or how to act.

"I am very sorry to hear that. They act very foolishly if they think to come against you."

"You are right! I am the head of the Church of England. How dare they defy me!" Henry was now roaring his displeasure, not caring if he woke the whole castle.

To her credit, Jane did not flinch away. She accepted his kiss when it came with what seemed like great forbearance.

"Husband, I am sure that you will quell this rebellion as your father squashed those that happened during his reign. It is common for the common folk to do this. Especially if they are misled."

"Misled?" He zeroed in on this.

Elizabeth closed her eyes. What was her sister saying? Had she stumbled upon something?

"Who would mislead my people into rebellion against me, my sweet?"

Jane looked wide-eyed. "I mean…they are simple folk and would not leave their shires unless they were lied to. Was it not so in the past? Could it not be so now?"

Henry nodded, kissing her again, this time on the mouth. "How very well you think, my dear. You are right though. I shall see every traitorous scum hanged for this betrayal. Have I not suffered for the welfare of this kingdom? Is this how they intend to repay me?"

Elizabeth couldn't help her gaze drifting toward the door. Would she be able to slip out unseen? Would it be rude? She was trying to calculate her chances when Jane spoke again.

"You should not trouble yourself. This is the work of your ministers. What can I do to help you, sir?"

"There is no one but me that can do this work. No one." He was looking down at her now, peeved. "What can you do?" His voice stressed the "can." "You know very well what you can do, madam."

He rushed out of her rooms, reminded that he was disappointed in her.

"Jane, never fear. He speaks out of anger." Elizabeth had not hesitated to rush to her side, patting her shoulder. It was strange to be comforting her older sister. She remembered a time not long ago when Jane had patted her shoulders. She was to be married shortly and had not been keen on leaving home.

"I know." Her voice had gone quiet again. Barely a whisper.

"You are stressed. I can see it on your face. Maybe it is because I feel the same, but don't worry yourself into sickness. All will be well."

Jane shrugged her off. "It is easy for you to say that. But I am not stressed. I am the most happy. The Spanish ambassador said I was." Her lips twisted into a cruel smile. "Ah, now I must stop for lack of time," she said, spotting something near the door.

Elizabeth whipped around to see the door handle being pressed down. Someone was on the other side.

"Come in. Her majesty is awake," she called, schooling her features into serenity.

None other than Jane Rochford, followed closely behind by Margaret Douglas, came into the room.

"We heard noise and leapt out of bed," Margaret said by way of explanation.

"So why aren't you in your night shift, then?" Elizabeth was quick to point out.

Margaret blushed, and Jane Rochford's knowing smirk told Elizabeth all that she needed to know.

"I wasn't asleep yet…I was…"

"You were praying." Jane Rochford finished for her.

Margaret nodded. She was not such a fool that she would dare give her any sign of gratitude for the intervention.

"Fetch the queen a cup of warm ale."

"Was there news?" Jane Rochford asked, her curiosity piqued at last. She wasn't asking Elizabeth; she was looking over her shoulder to Jane, perched up on the pillows.

"Yes, I am afraid so. It is bad news for my husband. But I hope we shall all be safe here."

"An attack?"

"A few troublemakers in the north," Elizabeth said.

"Ah." Jane Rochford did not look entirely convinced.

Margaret had gone around them during this time to stoke the dying fire with a poker. "Would you like me to call the maids to have a few more logs brought in, Your Grace?"

"No, this is fine. I am warm in bed. I shall try to sleep some more. It is not even dawn yet. Please, go rest, all of you." Jane was looking at her too.

Elizabeth ushered them out of her sister's chambers.

"Well, it will be all over the palace by the time we break our fast."

"I suspect so," Jane said. Her head was back on her pillow. "I feel so tired."

Elizabeth frowned in concern. "Are you sure I cannot get you anything?"

Her sister shook her head. "Sleep."

The word was like a command.

Elizabeth climbed under her own covers and tried her best to comply.

CHAPTER FIVE

E veryone had their eyes on the king.
It wasn't like before, when their gazes swept over him, wondering how to impress him, wondering what it would take for him to favour them above all others, wondering how many riches he might bestow upon them.

Now the gazes of the courtiers were fearful. They watched him, wondering about the security of their own lands, their own money. What would happen if the northerners succeeded in their quest?

No one seemed to believe that the rebels meant no harm. If they made it to London, Henry Tudor would not be left sitting on his throne. Some other heir to the English throne would be brought forth. Perhaps a king from one of the old families of England would emerge. Perhaps one of the sons of King Edward would spawn out of the ground again.

Tense couldn't begin to describe the mood at court.

Through it all Elizabeth had to follow behind her sister, pretending to be sweet and temperate. She looked toward Cromwell and his men and was not comforted to see their faces drawn and weary.

If they were worried too, then this was not a battle that could easily be won.

She found her food hard to swallow but forced it down, even though it caught in her throat and made her feel like she was choking.

Her brother had left court, readying the tenants on their lands to fight the rebels.

The Duke of Suffolk had gone as well, to take the king's army into battle.

Elizabeth had not been there when the king had said he would ride out himself to face these rebels, but she heard about it from Lady Jane Ashley.

She heard how one of his men put a hand on his arm and whispered to him that it would not be wise for him to leave the capital. Henry had shot her sister a furious look, as if it was all her fault he was not able to go riding at the head of his army.

It wasn't him, the king, but his third wife that was to blame for the lack of sons in his nursery.

Jane took it stoutly. Apparently.

Elizabeth had only heard the tale after.

They were walking in the gardens, Jane ahead of them all with Lady Mary on her arm.

The former princess had recently arrived at court, her formal pardon expedited due to the circumstances.

"They were worried that the rebels would capture

her and place her on the throne," Lady Ashley said, coming up alongside her.

Another lady behind them muttered her agreement. She too had heard this rumour.

"I think her father was just concerned about her well-being. Any father would bring their children closer to home in such a trying time," Elizabeth said, thinking of her own children.

"He didn't bring the other one, though," Lady Bray pointed out.

"She's out of the way. Daughter of a queen who was little more than a whore. No one would plot on her behalf. But Lady Mary…" Lady Ashley said.

"Is still a bastard," Lady Bray interrupted.

Elizabeth didn't want to correct them. She didn't want to seem like she knew more than she was letting on.

"Well, it is nice to have her at court," Elizabeth said to change the subject.

"You would think so. Your family are papists too, aren't you?" Lady Ashley turned a critical gaze to her.

Elizabeth frowned. "We are nothing of the kind. We've always been devout, but my family worships and believes what the king does."

Sniggers from behind her made her want to whip around and find out what was being said, but she kept her cool.

"Lady Ashley, you are being rude," Lady Bray said.

"Well, I mean it is common gossip what passed between Queen Jane and the Spanish ambassador. It's why the Spanish favoured the marriage so much...at first."

That was rather unnerving to hear.

"Why would they not favour the marriage still?"

Elizabeth regretted asking that but couldn't help her curiosity. She made sure to put an edge in her voice to let Lady Ashley know she was not to be meddled with.

"She showed that she wasn't going to be their puppet. Not that she could even if she tried," Lady Jane Rochford answered as she caught up to them, pausing to give a tilt of her head in greeting to Elizabeth. "The king doesn't listen to her like he did to his other wives."

"She doesn't seek to lead him or meddle in his affairs," Elizabeth corrected, though her hands had tightened into fists in her pockets.

"Smart of her. Everyone seems to think she's dim-witted, but perhaps she's not," Lady Rochford said.

"Would you like me to report on you? Your words are paramount to insult. The king could throw you into the tower." Elizabeth could not hold back her anger.

Her shrill laugh made even Jane and Mary up ahead turn and look their way.

"The king would not do it. I have more powerful friends backing me."

"And who are they? Do tell me of the imaginary friends that live in your head. Who would trust you with their secrets and work?"

"Lady Ughtred," Jane called out. "Will you not join me?"

Elizabeth bit back a curse. How had she let her get to

her again? This would be all over the court. She could only pray that people would be too busy worrying about the rebellion to care too much about the spat between two ladies-in-waiting.

She walked slowly and purposefully toward her sister, who looked ready to scold her as though she was a child that had been disobedient.

"What were you all discussing?"

"Nothing of importance," Elizabeth said, unable to meet her eyes.

"It was hard not to hear at least some of what you said…" Jane looked irritated.

"Then you must have heard some of what they were saying too." Elizabeth's anger flashed.

Jane sighed. Exasperated. "Why don't you go inside and take some time to pray and meditate on your failings?"

Elizabeth wanted to say something, but was this not ideal? She was angry with herself too.

She nodded, curtsying to the both of them, and left without another word to anyone.

"Why oh why can I not watch my tongue?" She hadn't meant to say it out loud but she had, just as none other than Gregory Cromwell came down the steps among a gaggle of other clerics and pages.

She blushed scarlet, cursing her luck, but stepped to the side, allowing them to get past.

Gregory stepped apart from them, telling the others to go on ahead.

Her cheeks burned even redder. She was sure he had

heard.

"Are you all right, Lady Ughtred?"

She took a moment to reply, unable to form the words or think of something clever to say to turn this whole situation around.

"No," she said at last, looking up into his deep dark eyes that she now saw were lighter in the light of day—almost grey.

"Is there anything I can do to help?"

She couldn't help but take him at face value.

"No, I am afraid you cannot. As you can see, I have become an expert at leading myself into situations where I leave mortified."

"I cannot imagine that," he said, stepping back as though to examine her.

"You are teasing me now," she said, feeling her irritation rise.

She looked left and right and saw that now they were perfectly alone.

"Well, if it helps, I think we both have the tendency to say the wrong thing at the wrong time. None of us is ever as clever as we think we are. It takes an intelligent person to realize that."

"Is that a compliment?"

"If you wish it to be."

He was almost shy, and her heart skipped a beat in her chest at the implication. But no, this was court. This was nothing more than a bit of friendly playacting.

"You have been kind to me. Please don't go repeating all you hear me say around court."

"I shall not," Gregory said with the seriousness of a man giving an oath.

"Then I shall sleep easier."

She turned to walk away from him, but his hand had reached out, catching her hand.

She froze at the contact, her blue eyes fixed on him before pulling away.

"Was there something else?"

"Do not think ill of yourself. No one is perfect, and if we set impossibly high standards for ourselves we will never reach them and always be disappointed."

"So it is best to just...what? Be happy with the mediocre?"

He smiled, as though knowing himself what that felt like. "It sounds impossible, but I am sure the peasant in the field without any higher aspirations than getting another meal is happier than the mightiest king."

She frowned. "You must not have been around many peasants."

"You see, I say the wrong thing all the time too," he said with a shrug. "But do listen to me. Don't be too hard on yourself."

"You speak as though you are much older than I am, but you cannot possibly be so unless your father has discovered the cure for mortality."

He threw back his head in laughter.

"I have not heard that said about my father, and there are so many rumours about him. Those in the north call him the antichrist come to Earth."

"I am sorry for that. It must be a lot for a man to live

up to."

He laughed again, and it made her smile in return.

"I'll be sure to let him know you said so. But as to your question, I am twenty-five."

"Ah," she said, slightly surprised. He seemed younger than that, and she was surprised to discover he was five years her senior.

"Shall I inquire about your age?"

"That would be impolite. Now I must go, and you must disappear back to your friends before you are missed."

"Worried about rumours?" he said, cocking his head to the side. "According to some, we have already entered marriage negotiations."

She gave him a half-smile and left without another word. Her mood was lighter than it had been a few moments ago. This was now the second time he had done that to her and she didn't know what to make of it.

As she walked into the queen's apartments, Gregory Cromwell was put out of her mind. If it weren't for the serious faces of the yeomen of the guard, then she would have chalked this up to a practice for a masque. But this was no theatrical performance.

A sobbing Margaret Douglas was surrounded by three guards while the remaining yeomen carried out a search of her rooms. Her trunks were emptied out on the carpet. Any scrap of paper was collected, filed away to be read and deciphered by some clerk no doubt. Fine silks, satins, and lace spilled over the floor, an ocean of colour.

Elizabeth pursed her lips, pretending to embody

some magisterial power.

"You ought to be careful. If those get damaged, the king will not be happy," she said.

"Be on your way, lady," the captain said, not sparing her a second glance.

Elizabeth could hear Margaret's whimpering, a sound so unlikely to come from the loud brash girl.

"What is going on here?" Elizabeth was one step away from putting her hands on her hips to scold them as she would scold her Henry or an errant maid.

"Be on your way. We have our orders." This time he sounded gruffer and sterner.

But Elizabeth did not waver or let herself be frightened.

"My sister, the queen, would want to know what is happening here and why one of her own ladies-in-waiting is being...arrested in this manner."

He seemed to pause at that but then shook his head.

"I have my orders. I am not to say a word. Please, be on your way," he said, more politely this time.

"I love him, but I have done nothing wrong, I swear it. Lady Ughtred, tell the queen, tell the king. Please, I beg you."

Elizabeth looked toward Margaret, who seemed to have finally gotten the courage to speak.

"I shall do what I can," Elizabeth said, not sure what to think of all of this.

She hoped this didn't show too much sympathy for the distressed woman. If she had indeed committed a great crime, then she shouldn't associate herself with her.

She moved past the spectacle toward her own room and sat down on the bed, waiting for everyone outside to leave before emerging again.

She wasted no time in returning to Jane's side with the news that Margaret Douglas, the king's own niece, had been arrested. What could she have done to deserve such a punishment?

One look from Jane silenced her though. Not far ahead of the gaggle of ladies was the king himself, in conference with a man wearing a heavy black cloak. Cromwell.

They were talking in hushed tones, so it was impossible to hear what was being said, but Elizabeth would bet a year's income that it had something to do with Margaret.

If she had to bet, she would say she was caught with her lover, but that was hardly crime enough to have her sent to the tower, was it? She wasn't married; it wasn't as though she had made a cuckold of her husband.

Jane maintained the appearance of being passive and meek, but as Elizabeth sat beside her on a garden bench, Jane whispered into her ear.

"I can tell by your expression that you heard. His majesty is furious with me. He blames me for the whole affair. Did you know of it?"

"Know what exactly?" Elizabeth hissed back, pretending to adjust her skirts.

"Of her supposed marriage to Thomas Howard."

"What?" Elizabeth was truly in shock now. "The duke?"

"No, of course not. Don't be ridiculous. Tommy Howard, the younger brother, he's the one who hangs around the court with nothing to do but write poetry all day. It's been going on for quite some time apparently. From before I was married."

"What? And it was kept secret for so long…how were they discovered?"

Jane never got the chance to answer. The king approached them, a grim disappointed look pasted on his face, with Cromwell at his heels. Elizabeth could see how distraught the king seemed. It was an affront to him that his own niece had behaved so poorly, but surely he wouldn't actually harm his own flesh and blood.

Out of the corner of her eye Elizabeth caught the motion of Lady Mary stepping away, seeking to disappear among the crowd. Elizabeth shouldn't make such assumptions.

"I shall have to bring some of your ladies in for questioning, madam. Perhaps in the future you shall be more diligent in your care of them. So far you have failed miraculously in your duty on all counts."

Jane curtsied so low to him she was practically on her knees before him.

"I shall do better, milord."

"Good, see that you shall. I cannot tolerate this sort of behaviour."

Jane opened her mouth as though she was about to say something, perhaps in defence of the secret couple, but Elizabeth pinched her to keep her quiet.

The king strolled past with his minister, who spared one glance her way. A tight-lipped smile.

Should she be flattered by the attention?

When they were gone, Jane rose from her position.

"Why did you pinch me?"

"I could sense you were about to do something foolish," Elizabeth said. "Was I wrong?"

Jane tilted her head, considering. "You are probably right, but how can I not say something for her? Poor thing. What will her mother say in Scotland?"

"She was a poor mother if she left her here alone."

"She wanted her to be safe," Jane said, contradicting her.

Elizabeth knew it was futile to argue with her. Jane wasn't a mother herself; she couldn't understand the sentiments of a mother.

"Well, what I would like to know is how this all came out," Elizabeth said, glancing around at the other ladies around them. They were all floundering about, most chatting among themselves, sharing any titbit of gossip they could.

"It was the duke that told the king, but he found out from Edward."

"What do you mean? Edward is up north."

"It was before he left. He met with Norfolk and asked him to keep an eye on his brother," Jane said with a shrug, as though it was as simple as that.

It wasn't, of course. Elizabeth bit the inside of her cheek. It had been she who had said something to Anne, who said she would speak to Edward, but he had not indicated he would do something like this. It irked her. But she supposed he wouldn't know how the king would react either. A sense of guilt washed over her. Margaret had asked for her help, but in fact she should have been cursing her for getting her into this mess in the first place.

The duke had chosen his timing poorly. He should have waited for the rebellion in the north to be crushed before bringing the king bad news. Then the king might have been merciful. One would think that family would protect each other, but the opposite seemed to be true of the Howards. What a family. But it was no wonder that they had spawned the likes of Anne Boleyn.

∽

A week passed and the rebels had forced their way into the city of York. The chapel bells rang all day in celebration. The details of how they had done so were vague. At least ten different stories were circulating around court, but it did not really matter how or when it occurred. What really mattered was that these rebels had taken the second-largest city in England.

Suddenly, the threat seemed all the more real.

She had finally heard from her brother, Edward, that he had escorted her children part of the way south.

She could breathe a sigh of relief that they were safe. Her father-in-law was likely making his way to London, and she would be reunited with her children.

The news for Margaret Douglas was not so good. Her lover had been locked up in the tower with her, but they were not allowed to see each other or even have paper for fear that they would send each other letters.

Word had it that they were questioned for three straight days. The examiners picked apart every story. In the end, Margaret Douglas was discovered to not have been married after all. However, Tom Howard had deflowered a royal lady, a crime punishable by death.

If any of the Howards minded or were trying to find some way to help a member of their family, it was not clear. When the duke had ridden north to meet the rebels, he had seemed as unconcerned as ever, pressing on with his business as usual.

Elizabeth said a prayer for Margaret, hoping that the foolish girl would be spared. She did not deserve such terrible punishment for her crimes. No matter what the king of England thought.

Daily the king was locked away in his privy chambers, discussing strategies and battle plans with his ministers and lords of the privy council.

Rarely did he come to Jane's room. On the odd occasion that he did, he never stayed long. Sometimes it was because of meetings, but other times it was clear to everyone that he was simply unhappy.

Then the king had no choice but to parley with the rebels and agree to their demands. Of course he couldn't bring himself to concede to absolutely everything, but he wasn't in much of a position to bargain.

He offered every man full pardon for their actions and promised to start a parliament in York and crown Jane there next summer. As a cherry on top of the proceedings, he invited Robert Aske, the leader of the rebellion, to London to spend Christmas with the court so they could iron out the details of the negotiations.

Elizabeth couldn't believe that the king would make such a concession. She had seen for herself how ruthless he could be.

She looked toward Cromwell, standing behind the king, an ever-present shadow. What of the demands to have Cromwell put on trial for his crimes? Would the king abandon his minister?

Her brother reappeared at court not long after this. The king's forces had been disbanded. Edward wore a tight-lipped expression, as if he knew something and was trying his best not to show his hand too soon.

"How were things?" she asked. "I know you always wanted a command of your own. Military glory and all that."

He merely shrugged. "There was no glory in this."

"Come on, Edward, don't be so hard on yourself," Elizabeth said, touching his elbow.

"Sister, I know you are just trying to pry for information in that way that you do. I cannot say anything now. Nor is there anything to say," he said with a tone of finality.

"I really was curious about how you did as a commander. I wasn't just prying for information."

"I'm glad. Otherwise, we wouldn't have been as close as we are."

She gave him a small smile but walked off. She was exhausted, but she had been having trouble sleeping.

Tomorrow she'd been given permission to ride out to see her children and spend a few days with them.

∽

A few blissful weeks of contentment passed. They were nearing the Christmas season and spirits were high. Depending on which side of the battle you were on, anxieties were as well.

"You Cromwells have made yourselves scarce," Elizabeth said, coming across Gregory on the way to chapel one morning. "I rarely see any of your father's livery around court these days."

His eyebrow rose in surprise at her frankness, but she did not let it deter her.

"Well?"

"My father thought it would be politically the best move. He is still here, still by the king."

"I know."

She was looking at him. She had come dangerously close to saying: "But I haven't seen you for quite some time."

"If you are so well informed, why bother asking me, then?"

"Perhaps I enjoy talking to you and was looking for an excuse," she said with the hint of a smile.

"You amuse me. I know you well enough to know that you are not some flirt who enjoys the game of courtly love."

She flattened the panels of her skirt with her palm.

"When did you get to know me so well?"

Now he looked evasive and ready to change the subject, but before he could she smiled and moved on.

"I am simply perplexed. The king has made promises, but I have not seen any plans being made for my sister's crowning, for example. I worry that the danger is not gone yet and that my children should not return north." She was speaking quietly. She didn't care about how it looked. Let people assume the worst. She'd rather have the information.

He frowned. "A lot of people are wondering the same thing. The king cannot keep up the pretence much longer."

Her eyebrows shot up in surprise. "I don't know what I expected. You don't know...if the king is planning to get rid of my sister, do you?"

"Oh, nothing like that. Your sister is safe. She is his beloved wife. Why would he have cause to get rid of her?"

The heat from her cheeks alerted her to the fact that she must have turned red from head to toe. How could she have made such a dangerous mistake? She turned away from his gaze, unable to meet it.

"He has no cause. I just feared... well, he has not crowned her yet."

Elizabeth wondered why she was making her thoughts so plain to him. It was dangerous to do so. Had she become addicted to the feeling of racing toward danger? But when she looked into his dark grey eyes she didn't feel anxious. In fact, it was quite the opposite.

With a sigh she moved to turn away, but he stopped her with a look.

"I cannot say anything, but I do not think we have seen the last of the troubles with the rebels. I make no claims to knowledge. Even my father does not tell me all of his plans. Does that make you feel better? Having that knowledge?"

He was clearly expecting her to say no or to run off scared. But she thanked him. "I like to be prepared. Come what may."

"I shall keep that in mind."

∽

A few weeks later, Margaret Douglas was still kept locked away in the Tower of London.

Elizabeth, like many others, was hopeful the king would show her mercy and release her. She was cynical enough by now to know that the king was not the ideal image of a perfect prince that he liked to portray himself as, but shouldn't he show kindness to his family?

Elizabeth worried, but not like the others worried. Her sister's life could be on the line. Her own brothers could get dragged into the machinations of the court if they decided to turn on them. They all pretended nothing was wrong. They all pretended that this wouldn't happen to them, but it had happened twice now.

The first time, the king had turned on the advisers who had dared disagree with him, punishing his wife of over twenty years by sending her into exile. The second time, he had turned against his wife and her family but was not content with disgracing them. He had ordered their heads chopped off. It was by now common knowledge that the king had ordered an executioner even before Anne Boleyn's trial. There was no justice in this kingdom.

Edward had laughed at her when she had even tried to hint at this, but really, what was stopping the king from turning his wrath on them?

She was beginning to wake every day in a panic. Watching the king every day for signs that he was displeased.

He had gotten over his initial anger over the Margaret Douglas affair. It was as though it had never happened.

Perhaps that coldness should have terrified her more.

It was reported that Robert Aske, the leader of the rebellion, would soon arrive in London.

The court was stunned.

First by the fact he had been arrested the minute he left the safety of his army, and then by the fact Aske would come at all.

Many thought this must be some farce to trick Aske into coming down within Henry's grasp. He could not forgive his own niece for some bit of folly, but he could turn the other cheek to someone who had taken up arms against him?

Elizabeth had heard Aske was a lawyer, but now she was sure he was also a fool. Who would walk willingly into the den of a lion?

The king had been smart. The rebels had professed they were not rising against him. They claimed to love him.

"Well, let them come and embrace me," he had said to his astonished council. "I will listen to them. If they put down their arms and plead my forgiveness, they shall find I am a merciful prince."

What could they do but accept the king's invitation? If Aske had not agreed, then the king would have said that they were truly godless rebels. There was no winning. By taking half measures they had lost.

If Elizabeth had been Aske, she would have come marching into London after taking York.

How far would the law of the land get him?

She would bet that Aske would meet a gruesome end. He wouldn't be allowed to live. This opinion she kept to herself. She kept her face serene and cool as she stood off to the side witnessing Aske make his bow before the king and the queen, her sister. Later on she had shuddered when she watched the king envelop Aske in his own red velvet cloak.

It seemed to her that the king was saying: you have been caught. You are mine. There is nowhere for you to run anymore.

She was so absorbed in the machinations of court, of watching Aske, the dead man walking, that she had not noticed how her sister had begun feeling unwell in the morning.

They were approaching the end of March and the last of the New Year celebrations was fast approaching with the Feast of the Annunciation. Elizabeth was helping Jane dress when she placed a cool hand on hers.

"I must talk to you, Elizabeth," she said in a low whisper.

Elizabeth nodded before walking behind her sister to begin pinning the gable hood in place. The little diamonds on the ends sparkled as they caught the early morning sunlight.

"Shall I send them away?" Elizabeth said. The other maids and ladies-in-waiting were loitering about.

"That would be too obvious. I find it is hard for me to ever be alone at all," she sighed.

Elizabeth could understand. There was no such thing as being alone at court. Even for her, a lady-in-waiting. She could count on her fingers the amount of time she had been in a room alone.

"I shall contrive some reason at some point today."

Jane tilted her head in acknowledgement and said no more.

There was something Elizabeth wanted to talk to her sister about too. Wasn't there some way that Jane could help her? She needed some financial security that didn't leave her relying on her brothers and family.

Finally, on their way out of the queen's chapel they got their chance. They were accosted by a troupe of musicians playing a lovely ballad written by the king for the queen. The music was loud and everyone was distracted by the antics of the king's fool.

Jane leaned closer to her, as though making some commentary on the performance.

"My courses have not come and I have been feeling sick in the mornings. Is that how it was with you?"

Elizabeth's breath hitched in her throat. She had to use every inch of strength she possessed to maintain her composure.

"Yes. Are you certain?"

"As certain as one can be."

Elizabeth dared to look at her sister and saw her smile was tight and forced.

"You must tell the king."

"Should I not wait and be certain?"

"No." Elizabeth did not hesitate. To seem uncertain would cast doubts. The king might wonder why Jane was concerned. He might get suspicious, and that was all he would need to launch a full inquiry. Who knew what the enemies of the Seymours might dredge up?

There was a blast of trumpets and fanfare as the musicians concluded their song to the applause of the audience. Jane clapped loudest of all before motioning to a lady-in-waiting behind her to hand them a coin.

"I'll tell him it is a possibility," she said at last.

Elizabeth had the urge to argue with her, but she had to fight her instincts. There was already a high chance they had been overheard. It wasn't just Jane Rochford they had to watch out for. Any of Jane's many attendants could be ready to report on her. Many were likely in the pay of many others. She wouldn't be surprised if the laundry maids were being paid a pretty penny these last few months.

Everyone wanted to know whether or not her sister

was with child. If she had more sense and could hide her name, she would roll up her sleeves and tie her hair up and head down to the laundry herself. It would be more lucrative for her.

The jubilant mood was not cut by the arrival of the traitorous northern lords either. The king was visibly cool with them, but still they weren't whisked away to the tower and a traitor's death. At least not yet.

Elizabeth was distracted by the reappearance of her would-be lover Arthur Darcy. He had arrived at court to account for his father's actions, but the seriousness of his mission did not stop him from making the occasional remark. From giving her a knowing smirk every time he saw her.

Did he imagine she had warmed to his advances?

She shuddered.

During one of many banquets, he asked her to dance and she could not find a reason to refuse, not with so many eyes upon her.

"It has been a long time since I have seen you," he said, as though to imply he missed her.

"Has it really? I can't recall."

This snide comment did not seem to dampen his spirits.

"You ought to be careful. I was hoping I might find you more amenable. I heard your brother was raised to be a viscount. You have become a more attractive prospect for me."

Elizabeth bit her inner cheek, grateful that the dance

had her turn away from him at just that moment. What a fool he was.

"I am happy you think so, but I am not on the lookout for another husband, despite what you may have heard or think," she said.

The song was ending and he drew her away to walk with him, but she had no reason to continue the conversation.

"As flattered as I am sure any woman would be, you must realize by now that I will not marry you. I have no intention of doing so. I hope you will do me the honour of respecting my wishes."

He opened his mouth to say something, but she didn't give him a chance and curtsied to him, pulling her hand away from him before turning tail and returning to her sister's side.

Serving her sister had become a refuge. No one would dare pull her away from there. Except perhaps her own brothers.

As she walked back up to the high table, making her curtsies to the king and her sister, she spotted Gregory Cromwell watching her. He looked away as soon as she noticed him.

It must be telling to all the northern lords that the king had chosen a Cromwell to be his cupbearer this night. Or maybe they had not realized since he bore very little resemblance to his father.

"How are you, sister?" Elizabeth asked, leaning close to her.

Jane turned a jubilant face toward her. "Very well. I have no appetite."

The two statements were so contradictory, but Elizabeth understood what she was saying. She wanted desperately to ask her if she had said anything to the king.

She looked more closely at him. He did have an air of contentment about him. His hand holding Jane's.

It was probably a safe bet to assume that she had.

Her heart swelled with happiness for her sister.

"What can I get you? You should eat something."

"I've been eating some bread," Jane said with a shrug.

Elizabeth thought back to her own pregnancies. With her second she had been hardly able to eat anything, even less so keep anything down.

"Try to pretend at least. Or force yourself to eat a bit, especially meat. It's good for the baby, and you don't want anyone talking."

Jane nodded. "I am very happy."

"As anyone would be. Shall I say something to our brother?"

Jane tilted her head slightly, motioning that she could.

Elizabeth did not get a chance to have a private word with her brother until the next day. She had wanted to be as inconspicuous about her news as possible. She didn't want the whole court to know that the Seymours had reason to be so happy and rush to each other with the news.

Anne Stanhope was holding her baby, examining his chubby little cheeks when she came in.

"Good morning, sister," Elizabeth said, fighting back the pang in her chest. She missed holding her own child. "How is little Edward today?"

"He's growing well. Edward is sending him to Oakham Hall. He's set up a proper nursery for him. The court is no place for him."

"It is hard, I know." Elizabeth was sympathetic. No wonder Anne was being so doting right now.

"It's a wonderful thing for him. He will grow up in the clean country air with tutors and anything a boy like him would need," Anne continued.

Elizabeth walked over to her, placing a hand on his little head. He squirmed a bit, his lips grimacing as though he was ready to cry, but she smiled down at him and cooed before placing a tender kiss on his forehead and saying a blessing.

"And you can visit him whenever you like." Elizabeth felt the need to remind Anne.

"Yes, of course." Then it seemed as though something dawned on her and she looked sheepishly at Elizabeth. "I am sorry you cannot be with your children."

"I could, but duty calls. I had many good years with them and will have many more still. When Jane no longer needs me, I will retire to the country."

"Your family would never let you go. They are planning some sort of great marriage for you."

"That would be news to me," Elizabeth said, though she wasn't concerned. The days when her brothers could bully her were long gone. At least she hoped so. "But tell me, where is Edward? I wish to speak to him. I have news."

"Good, I hope. He's been in a mood. The king called him and a few other trusted lords into the council chambers a few days ago, and they were talking for hours. He came out pale and angry."

Elizabeth could see that Anne was perplexed. "He did not hint to you what was to happen?"

"No, he didn't say a word about it, and when I pressed him he told me to mind my business. Well, you can bet I gave him a talking-to."

"Good," Elizabeth said with an amused smile. It always made her laugh to see how her sister-in-law so obviously ran the household. Perhaps Edward was too in love to gainsay her, but he wasn't that type of man. He wasn't a man like the king to fall passionately in and out of love.

Timely, as always, Edward chose to appear right then and there.

"You two look like you are conspiring."

Elizabeth shot him a look of disapproval.

"I wanted to talk to you," she said, then heard a little cough beside her. "And you too, of course," she said with a tilt of her head to Anne.

"What is it?"

Elizabeth could see how tired Edward looked. He seemed deflated somewhat. She hoped to be able to pick his brain, but she doubted he would be forthcoming if he had not even talked to his own wife.

"It is good news." She decided to reassure the both of

them.

Anne placed Edward in the hands of his waiting nurse and dismissed her. "I think the little lord is hungry."

Once they were gone, Edward invited her to continue with a sweep of his hand. "Well?"

"Jane suspects she is with child. She has told the king, I think."

Edward's face lit up. "I had no doubts that God would bless our sister. I am to be the uncle to the Prince of Wales!"

He was as jubilant as he had been on the day his own son had been born.

Elizabeth shared a knowing glance with Anne. The same thought had seemed to occur to them at once.

What if the child was not a boy but a girl? They doubted there would be much rejoicing then.

Edward had not missed their expressions. "Could it be anything else but a prince for England?"

What could she say? She was no fortune-teller.

"The surest way to find out is to wait for the birth. The king's astrologers have been wrong in the past. I wouldn't put much credence in them."

Edward frowned. He did not seem to like being told something potentially unpleasant.

"I am sure all will be well." Anne decided to chime in. "This is a true marriage blessed by God with no impediment. The whole country prays for the king to have a son. God will hear all of our prayers."

"Yes." Edward seemed reassured. "Jane has not a sin

to her name. At least not...well...this is cause for celebration. We shall hold all the cards in our hands now. We must think of how to use this to our advantage."

He turned a smiling face to Elizabeth. A mischievous grin on his face. "I am sure Arthur Darcy would be more than pleased to be married to you now."

"Let him be disappointed, then. He has missed his chance with me." Elizabeth was readying herself for a fight, but Edward held up his hand.

"Peace, sister. I would counsel you against a match with him even if you were so inclined. But I do like seeing you ready for a fight."

"I don't know if I appreciate it."

The tense moment was broken by their laughter.

Without realizing it, the mood in the room had shifted to one of joyous celebration. Elizabeth was feeling particularly jubilant. More optimistic. There was nothing indeed that could possibly stand in the way of her family's happiness.

"But why would you counsel me against a marriage to Darcy?" She looked to Anne, who seemed to have fixated on the same issue.

Edward, caught out by them, scratched at the back of his head. There was something he was holding back. He was keeping secrets, that much was obvious, but Elizabeth tried to judge the likelihood of his divulging them.

She remembered her conversation with Gregory Cromwell and a thought struck her. Like puzzle pieces that finally fit together she came to a realization.

"Is the king planning to move against the rebels?"

"No."

His answer had come too quick, and he knew it too. Anne looked at him, shocked.

"You kept such important news from me?"

Elizabeth ignored her. She couldn't take her eyes off him. He had gone pale.

"I must swear you both to secrecy. My life, your lives would depend on it. Swear now. I will say nothing, but you must stop asking me about…that."

"I swear by all that is holy," Elizabeth said, Anne followed suit.

Edward deflated, collapsing into a chair.

"I don't want to do it, but I must since I have been named to the king's privy chamber. I cannot say what I must do, but it weighs heavily on me."

"Then let's leave it at that," Anne chimed in, the cheerfulness in her tone as false as the promise of a king. "How far along does Jane think she is?"

"It's hardly likely that she's missed more than one of her courses."

Anne's expression twisted into amusement as she seemed to realize how foolish her question was.

"Well, let us have a toast to Queen Jane. May she continue on in health and prosperity," Edward said. He had gone off to the side cupboard and was pouring them watered-down wine into three cups.

They toasted her sister, but Elizabeth was feeling her excitement give way to anxiety once more. What was going on with the rebellion? All would be well with her sister, wouldn't it?

The news spread around court, quietly at first. Then, by the time Jane had missed her monthly courses again, the news had spread to the city. There was no official announcement, but the mood at court had turned once more to real joy and excitement.

Elizabeth was sure there were just as many people wishing them joy as there were people wishing them ill luck, but no one dared to openly scorn them.

To do so now would-be treason. It would be questioning the king's potency, and one man had already lost his head for merely suggesting it.

Jane's appetite waxed and waned with each passing day, until Elizabeth was growing ever more concerned. Her sister needed to eat properly to feed the child growing within her.

"Is there nothing you would prefer to eat?

Jane looked pensive for a moment. Then it seemed to dawn on her.

"I want to eat quail eggs."

"Eggs?" Elizabeth's eyebrow arched. "Well, you should have said so. You don't want to waste away, do you?"

Jane shrugged, as though the thought hadn't occurred to her. She had become serene these last few days, but Elizabeth suspected it was because she was tired and not sleeping well at night. The child was making her feel nauseous day and night.

"I shall tell the kitchens to send you up as many quail's eggs as you will eat."

"Thank you," Jane said, a hungry look in her eye, almost as though she was salivating.

∽

With the negotiations long over, Aske had begun his journey back north to keep his side of the bargain and disperse his army. Elizabeth had been among the crowd when he was bid farewell by the king himself. Aske had been made aware of Jane's condition, and he bowed low and kissed her hand. The news would spread that this time it seemed as though the king's marriage was blessed.

Elizabeth knew that was his intention, but he always seemed to forget that this was not the first time that one of the king's many wives had been pregnant. Most had not ended happily.

As Aske departed, Cromwell seemed to miraculously reappear. He was never really gone. Elizabeth couldn't imagine the king could survive without him for long at this point.

She wondered if Aske knew or if he foolishly took the king at his word. He was a fool indeed if he did.

Time would tell.

Whatever had been the king's plan, he managed to make the rebels disperse. Perhaps he simply wanted to buy some time. He knew the cold winter weather would drive the fight out of most of the rebels. He knew that the longer they stood around waiting, the more bored they would become, or their fears and anxiety would overcome their confidence.

Even as Aske travelled north, the great pilgrim army had begun dispersing.

He had sent word ahead to his generals that he had the king's assurances that all promises made on the battlefield would be kept. Aske ordered that the army disband in order to show the king that they were upholding their end of the bargain.

He was home for barely a month before Norfolk's men dragged him from his home and arrested him, despite the king's pardon in his pocket.

He was blamed for the most recent uprising, even though he had taken no part in it. Some people who had been less naive and trusting than him had tried to revive the rebellion yet again. This time the Duke of Norfolk had been ready and did not hesitate to squash this rebellion quickly before more people rallied to the cause. The king used this as an excuse to have Aske and other rebel leaders imprisoned. Their trials were a foregone conclusion.

Aske, a lawyer by trade, was baffled by the turn of events, baffled that the piece of paper with the king's signature and seal meant nothing.

Elizabeth could not laugh at him. She pitied him but never dared voice this.

The king's wrath did not stop with Aske. It crept over his realm, snatching at any who may have participated in such insurrection.

Lords and common folk alike were imprisoned.

Arthur Darcy disappeared from court to be replaced by his father. Unlike his son, Tom Darcy possessed a steady character. He was old but steady, and even as he was jailed in the Tower of London for joining the rebels, he did not waver in his respect and proper comportment.

Even the protestant sympathizers pitied him.

It should have been a happy time. Jane's pregnancy was progressing well. She finally regained some of her appetite, but the king seemed keen on showing his people who was in charge. He wanted to punish all the people who dared oppose him. He wanted every man and woman who took part in the rebellion, or even assisted the rebels in some way, to hang.

Elizabeth was terrified to be around the king nowadays, but she was also too scared to leave her sister's side. Her brother, who was put as one of the judges, became withdrawn, not talking to anyone.

He clearly did not enjoy hounding men to their deaths. He did not enjoy passing judgment on men that carried the king's pardon in their hands. How could he face them as they said they had thrown themselves on the king's mercy and were given forgiveness and their liberty? It was Edward who had to say that this was not so, that the king called them traitors and would see them suffer as such.

There was no kindness in the king. No pleas for mercy would stay his hand. Only seeing Jane and her growing belly made him smile. But her presence merely proved to confirm that he was right. God was showing him His favour.

Jane often seemed on the precipice of speaking to the king about stopping his tirade. Elizabeth watched her with some anxiety, praying that she wouldn't be brave enough to raise the subject.

The king might forgive her for now, since she was carrying his child, but he would remember, and the minute he began having any doubts Elizabeth could see how easily her sister would end up in the tower as well.

They were having a family conference. Thomas, Henry, and Edward were present, and Anne was there as well. They spoke about mundane things at first, their sister's health and plans for the summer, before they turned to her.

"It would be a good time now for you to find another husband," Thomas said.

Elizabeth was taken aback; she had not been paying attention.

"I am not on the market."

"We have everything to play for now. Jane is with child. You are the aunt to the future king of England, and Edward can add more to your dowry."

Elizabeth looked perplexed but looked away from Thomas to Edward. "Why would you wish me to hurry into another marriage now?"

"It would be a good thing for the family, to create new alliances and bonds for the time to come. You are a more attractive prospect now."

Elizabeth was sure he was trying to compliment her and reassure her, but he had seemed to forget everything she had ever said to him.

"I do not wish to marry."

"You may not have another chance. We need more friends." Thomas was less tactful than Edward. "There is a very real chance the king will be displeased with us, with Jane, and our star may fall. We need to have allies."

"If you've made enemies, then that is not my fault. I never agreed to pawn myself off. You act as though Jane would anger the king. You seem to take that as a certainty. I am shocked that my own family would have such little faith." Elizabeth crossed her arms in front of her. She wished herself away from here.

"There are many that wish us ill. There are many who wonder why the king married Jane. We want to be prepared for that time."

"You are dangerously close to suggesting there is anything to worry about. I will not be sold again."

"Pick the man yourself then, as long as he comes from a good family and will stand our friend. We are a small family from nowhere. Do you think the Duke of Norfolk does not wish to find someone else from the Howard clan to sit on the queen's throne?"

Elizabeth shook her head. "I am freshly widowed. It would be improper."

"It has been over a year. But we are not rushing you. It is your duty and you cannot stay single for long. You must do this to help us. You will see reason."

Elizabeth frowned. She was being treated as though she was a child. But she wasn't some ignorant young woman who dreamt of knights and a happily-ever-after. Marriage brought struggles, and though she had been lucky in her husband, it could have ended so differently for her.

She had been hoping to live her life in quiet obscurity until she would be too old to be of notice to anyone. She rose from the table.

"You will excuse me. I seem to have some husband hunting to do." She let the sarcasm drip with every word.

She knew that her brother was right, but her heart fought against it. She wasn't about to throw herself into another marriage, but if she took matters into her own hands, perhaps things could be on her terms, more or less.

The next few days she went through all the eligible bachelors one by one in her head. Weighing their pros and cons. If they had known what was going on, they might have turned and run. It amused her to judge them as one would a horse for sale at the market. What could they offer her? She found most wanting, or she was too uncertain about their characters and temperaments.

Then an idea struck her.

It was a devilish idea. She looked over toward the gentlemen of the king's privy chamber. The Cromwell men were littered among them, but Gregory was not there. He did not have an official position at court, so that was unsurprising. The difficulty would be finding him without being so obvious about it. When his father was hiding away at court, he had become his messenger.

She looked away, back at the needlework in her lap, trying to think more rationally. It would be a match many would scoff at, but the truth was Cromwell was a powerful man at court and had made himself indispensable to the king. He held a lot of political power, even if it was not obvious. His son did not seem to possess the same devilish spirit. He had been raised in the house of gentlemen and educated as one. He was even known to partake in the joust. The few times they had interacted he had seemed...nice. His company was enjoyable.

This could be a good match. One she could tolerate, one where she might gain some power and influence while at the same time showing her family she was not to be meddled with. He was not terribly old either. On the other hand, people might laugh at the Seymours stooping so low. But who else could she marry to rival the power of the Howards? Why not go to the most powerful man of the kingdom, second only to the king?

She bit her lower lip. This would be difficult indeed.

Would her brothers even approve? They still needed to give her permission. It would need to seem like it was their idea. Then there was another matter.

Would her prospective bridegroom even want to marry her? His father was likely looking at several candidates for him. What would Cromwell want with a poor widow like her?

"Is that needlework giving you trouble?"

Elizabeth looked up to see Catherine Bilney looking down at her work. Elizabeth forced a little half-smile.

"Yes, I can't seem to focus on it. My mind keeps drifting."

"The honeysuckles are beautiful. You and your sister are expert needlewomen," Catherine said, with a bit of jealousy twinging her voice.

"There was nothing to do in the country but practice. I could show you this pattern if you want," Elizabeth offered.

Catherine took a seat beside her, but she seemed more intent on gossiping than learning her craft.

This was why it could be hard to get anything done.

Catherine had much to tell her though, including the fact that she had received a letter from Margaret Douglas.

"Have you received one? I was her friend, but I do not know what she expects me to do. I have no influence at court."

"Perhaps she just wants to hear from her friends. It is good that she is allowed to send and receive letters again though."

"Well...I hope so. But it's not my fault if I receive a secret letter from her."

"It would be if you go around spreading it everywhere."

Catherine blanched at that. "You have a point. I said nothing, then. But I am sure that things are improving for her. Tom Howard died in the tower. There is nothing to offend the king any longer. Even if they were married, she would be a widow now."

Elizabeth nodded. This made sense, but the king was not in a forgiving mood currently. She was sure it would suit him just fine to keep his niece locked up. Maybe he had even forgotten about her. He seemed prone to forgetting the women of his family.

The discussion of Margaret Douglas did not dampen her spirits overmuch. She became fixated on finding a way to speak to Gregory Cromwell. Just as she was beginning to get desperate enough to march to the Cromwell rooms and ask to see him, a risky move by any means, she finally saw him while they were on a ride with the king.

A long winter was finally giving way to spring, and it was an abnormally warm day. The king wished to take advantage of the good weather and left Jane to her rooms with a kiss on her forehead.

He had explicitly invited Mary Shelton to come along with him, and the whole court knew what that meant.

With a grimace, Edward suggested that she might like to join the party too.

"I don't want there to be talk, and perhaps if you are there the king might remember Jane."

"He has never not found mistresses, especially while his wives were with child. Why concern yourself over this?"

"I don't want this to be a Howard plot. We must be vigilant."

"I thought with Jane pregnant our troubles were over."

Edward shook his head. "Only after she gives birth to a son. Then we would be safe. But now everyone else is trying to make a play in case she fails. They are ready with their poison."

With a final shrug, Elizabeth agreed to go. Her brother was fooling himself if he thought she could stop the king from doing anything he wanted.

Norfolk had ridden through his lands, visiting every

town and village to root out rebels and hang them. Gossipmongers said that half the north was hanging from the trees. The imagery sent terror through Elizabeth at such disturbing news.

Mounted on Jane's grey hunter, she wore a borrowed dark-green riding cloak. It was hard not to enjoy the beautiful weather. The sun felt warm on the nape of her neck.

The hunting party set out. The baying dogs and hunting calls made it hard to hear anything, much less have a conversation, but when Elizabeth spotted Gregory riding ahead she knew this was her chance.

She dug her heels into the horse's side, urging him to run faster.

It took some clever manoeuvring on her part to be able to seem to appear by his side.

He looked surprised to see her and even more surprised when she smiled up at him and the words came pouring out of her mouth. She was quick and to the point. There was no time for any bashfulness on her part.

She could see the slight red spreading over his cheeks and wasn't sure if it was from the wind. She didn't flatter herself to think he was blushing out of happiness at the prospect of marrying her.

"Tell me your answer or find a way to contrive to speak to me. I don't have much time. But if you are amenable, perhaps you might suggest to your father to speak to my brothers."

"You are serious, then? This wasn't some joke thrown together by you ladies?"

"I am serious. You once told me you prefer to live in the country. If this is true, then I think we would be more compatible than you think. I would be a good and loyal wife to you. I don't ask for much. I think we could get along and perhaps solve many problems. I have proven I am fertile, so your father could have no concerns there."

"You drive a hard bargain. What is it that you want in return?" He still talked as though they were jesting.

"I want my family's protection. I know your family, or your father, could provide it."

He frowned. "He is unmarried. Why not propose yourself to him?"

It was Elizabeth's turn to redden. "I wouldn't dream of it."

"So you think perhaps I am the more easily influenced?"

He was frowning now, looking at her with more suspicion than amusement. She was quick to shake her head.

"I...I simply enjoy your company more, and that is not me being coy. Am I wrong when I think we could be happy together? We seem to share the same interests, and we can tolerate each other's presence to hold a conversation."

"You set a very low bar for a man to meet."

"You'd be surprised by how few seem to pass even such low expectations." Elizabeth knew her time was running out. Her brother up ahead was looking around for her. "Well, think about it. My family is pushing me to marry. I don't have much time."

He tilted his hat toward her, and with that she spurred her hunter forward, leaping over a small log that sat across their path. She was comfortable in the saddle. She had been taught since she was very young that any accomplished lady could ride well enough to keep up with the men.

Later that night she wondered at her nerve to speak to him so forwardly. She half-expected it to be spread around court, something for Gregory to laugh at with his friends.

Luck was on her side because it seemed nothing had happened. A day passed and then another. Then a different sort of doubt began creeping in. Perhaps he had thought about it and did not wish to pursue it.

That was his right, and after that brazen display she wouldn't be surprised if he thought she wasn't worth the trouble.

But then, to her happy surprise, her brother asked to speak to her about a matter of some delicacy.

"Sit down, sister."

And she obeyed, watching him pace about his office.

"I don't know how to say this to you..."

"Perhaps start at the beginning. I find that always helps."

"An offer has been made. Some hints of an interest have been made toward you. You don't have any prospects of your own, do you?"

She shook her head, lying, but wishing him to get on with whatever he had to say.

"Cromwell invited me to dine with him yesterday

evening. He suggested something...and I—I know how you feel about him, sister. But it is a good match."

"Edward, I am sorry, you are confusing me and babbling. What is it that you have to say to me?" Elizabeth's heart was beating faster. Had she succeeded? Why was her brother running circles around the issue?

"He has proposed that you marry his son Gregory. I know his low birth would be objectionable to you, but this would be a great alliance for our family."

Elizabeth held up her hand to stop him.

"Edward, I do not care about his low birth. We aren't so high up ourselves. Who are we to turn our noses up at such a chance?"

"Yes, but we aren't lowly country knights anymore…"

"It is a gamble that Cromwell is willing to take. He could end up becoming related to a great family, or we could fall like so many others fell before us." She shrugged. "Who knows what will happen? The die has been cast."

Edward froze, his mouth hanging open slightly before recovering his wits.

"You surprise me, and I forget how pessimistic you can be."

"You are the one who encouraged me to find a husband soon while I have good chances of procuring a good match. If I am pessimistic, then so are you."

He inclined his head, acknowledging her point. "You are not wrong. So does this mean you will have him?"

She nodded, unable to meet his eye.

"I thought I would have to fight and argue with you," he said, scratching his head.

"Is that why we are having a private conference?"

"Well, Anne tends to be rough in her dealings with you." He smiled and it was the first time he had in a while. "She loves me too well to let someone, even my sister, upset me."

"You mean she spoils you. But on this matter we are in agreement. I will marry Gregory Cromwell."

Now his eyes narrowed into slits. "It's still all too easy. Are you sure this isn't some plan you've concocted yourself? Some trickery?"

"I cannot lie to you and say I have never spoken to him before, but there is nothing actually between us. I just believe that this is a good chance for me, and my chance at happiness with him is likely to be greater than with any other man I know. I never even met my first husband and yet I married him. So…"

Edward patted her shoulders, almost as though to say sorry for the way of the world. The gentiles were not of that sect of society that could just marry for love.

Noblemen and women married to please their families and do their duty.

"We shall tell the family, and with the king's permission you may be wed soon," he said with a wide smile. Some of the worries on his shoulders seemed to have been lifted.

Elizabeth hadn't been aware she was such a burden.

Within the week it was known that she was engaged to be married to none other than Gregory Cromwell.

The news distracted the insipid gossips from the more real tragedies going on up north. It was boring to talk of peasants being hanged when there was a lady being offered up on the chopping block to the grandson of a butcher. Or had he been a blacksmith? The rumours were unclear.

It was tantalizing for the courtiers to come up with all sorts of sordid tales of how her brother was forcing her to marry him in order to secure Cromwell's favour. Or that her brother had racked up a considerable amount of debt and offered her hand in marriage.

Elizabeth knew that the people could not be the most financially minded individuals themselves. For they had greatly overestimated her value. She had little to offer by way of a dowry, and she had been previously married and could no longer be considered young. Her family, though growing in the king's estimation, was not a very ancient or powerful one.

But it would be pointless to point this out. They would not understand.

Even those who did not laugh or question the marriage looked on it with pursed lips. It was not to their tastes to see a noblewoman betrothed to a commoner. It did not seem to matter to these people that Thomas Cromwell was Lord Privy Seal and had been made a baron. He could not escape his parentage.

Elizabeth felt pity for Gregory, who was labelled the villain. Though that alternated between him and his father. She thought the engagement would be called off for certain, but the Cromwell clan seemed to be well versed in handling the scorn of society.

They did not bat an eye at a stray comment.

What did it matter that someone laughed at their lack of noble blood? These were the same people that relied on them to keep their creditors at bay. They had enough power to destroy them, despite their common blood.

For the first time perhaps, Elizabeth understood the sort of family she was entering. This was a tight-knit clan that worked together to dangerous effect.

They did not play by others' rules. They made the rules.

It had been an awkward three days of questioning by the various ladies in her sister's chambers. Elizabeth often looked toward Jane and wondered if this was why she adopted such a dazed look, as though she could not hear what was being said to her.

It would have been easier to play dumb. Or perhaps easier to have picked someone safer to marry.

Why had she settled upon Gregory? The reasoning behind it grew dimmer in her own mind with each passing day. Had it really been a passing fancy? Perhaps a whim. Maybe she had chosen a name at random.

Then they were invited to dine at the Cromwell house in the city of London.

Like some blushing first-time bride, she realized how nervous she was as they took the barge downriver. Her heartbeat was irregular, her palms sweaty. She was a fool to have even spoken to Gregory at all.

She cursed herself over and over again. Even as she made her curtsy to her future father-in-law.

Now that he was here in his own home, greeting her as a future member of their family, he seemed more at ease. That sense that he might strike at you at any moment was no longer there.

Or maybe she was fooling herself.

She had dressed in a tawny gown edged with black fur against the cold air on the river. Her brother had accompanied her to this crucial dinner. They were here to iron out the terms. Man to man.

Elizabeth could have rolled her eyes when she heard them say that, but she did not argue. There were some spaces where even she did not wish to tread. She did not wish to break with all traditions. After all, it had been she who had proposed the marriage in the first place.

She did her best not to look about the room as though she was searching out her intended, but when their eyes met she couldn't help the playful smile that spread across her face. He nodded his head toward her.

So they were in agreement, then. Let the heads of the household think they had been pulling the strings in this arrangement all along.

Musicians played for them as they sat across the room from each other, chattering about nonsensical things. A tray of sweetmeats was laid before her, but she could not bring herself to touch it, as hungry as she was.

Then they were invited to the dining hall, a large stone room that may have been large enough to hold a mass inside.

"I know what you are thinking," Gregory, sitting on her right, said. "And you would be right. My father renovated the old parish church that was nearby and built an addition to connect this place to our old family home."

Her mouth parted in an "O," but no words came out.

"Are you the religious sort of woman?" he asked. "It's all right if you are, but I figured I shouldn't keep secrets from you and you ought to know where exactly you are dining.

"I am grateful for the knowledge, but I don't know how I can answer that sort of question."

"I find it hard to believe I have managed to silence you so quickly. I was half-expecting we jump into a theoretical debate before the venison is served."

"Whatever do you mean?" She couldn't meet his eyes as her hands skimmed the embroidered tablecloth. "This is very fine work."

"My mother's. She kept a shop. Sold embroidery until my father rose high enough in the cardinal's favour and she had a household to manage."

Her eyes snapped up to his.

"Are you surprised by how unashamed I am of my past?"

She shook her head, a bit at a loss for words. She wasn't any better than those gossiping courtiers, she supposed. "I am not. You must let me explain. It is wonderful to hear a man speak so kindly of his mother."

"I suppose it is not fashionable, but I cannot forget the love she had for us all, and you see my baseborn tendencies come out every once in a while. But it is expected of me..."

"I am sorry. For all the trouble this has caused. I did not think people would rattle on so about something as mundane as an engagement," she said.

He placed a hand over hers for the briefest of moments. "You are hardly mundane. Sister to a queen, marrying into the most infamous family in England."

"And, apparently, to a braggart," she said with a teasing smile. She was surprised to find herself relaxing around him.

He raised his glass in salute. "I am proud of our accomplishments, I suppose, though I do not wear our past like a badge of honour. My father is excessively proud of the fact he was born a common man. I am somewhere in the middle. I don't go around pretending I am something I am not. It would make it easier to fit in at court though. The old families don't like...upstarts."

"Who cares about them when you have the king's favour?" Elizabeth pointed out, despite knowing how naive that could sound.

Gregory shrugged, motioning for a server behind them to refill her cup.

The cup was of fine crystal and heavy in her hand. It would cost a fortune to own even one of these, and yet every diner had one at their seat.

The display of wealth was truly astounding.

"My father thinks of such things too. That is why he was keen on this marriage," Gregory said, in that way of his. "Let us mingle with the nobility, he declared."

Elizabeth couldn't quite stifle her laugh, and a few heads turned her way.

"You make us sound like we are the ones to be avoided," she said with a challenge in her voice.

"Your track record precedes your race. Time will be the judge."

She took a moment to sip her drink. She was enjoying their conversation, which should have been off-putting to her. She didn't want to jump into marriage or be excited about shackling herself to yet another man. But...the thought struck her that she needed to clarify things with him.

"You don't regret this arrangement?" she said under her breath. "You don't have to do me the kindness of marrying me. I feel as though I pushed you into something you weren't interested in."

"Were you keen on your first marriage?"

She frowned. "No, I cannot say I was, but I did go willingly if that's what you mean."

"You could not force me to do anything, so rest assured on that account. But I would call myself optimistic about our prospects. There were plenty of worse options to take. So overall, I would bet that we have as much chance of marital bliss as any other betrothed couple. Perhaps more so, for we already seem to be able to tolerate each other's company," he said with a wink.

She drained what was left in her glass in an effort to hide her embarrassment.

"We do seem to enjoy shocking each other with our blunt speech. But you are right and your words put me at ease...I would not wish to think you regretted agreeing to marry me."

The music in the hall had dimmed. Dish after dish was brought in. Elizabeth finally found she was able to eat.

Their conversation had not gone unnoticed, but there was nothing her brothers could do to reprimand her. Should she not talk to her soon-to-be husband?

The rest of the evening seemed to fly by quickly without much chance for them to speak properly again.

The date for her marriage was set for June. They had not asked for her opinion on the matter, but they did pause for a moment, just long enough for her to interject if she had been so inclined. To her it did not matter, and it would not suit the purposes of this marriage to prolong things further. Jane's baby was due in the fall, so it was better to conclude this marriage before then. Spring and summer were a common time for marriages to take place, so why wait another year?

The thought had occurred to her that perhaps her children could somehow be brought to live with them at their new home. That would be ideal, but she felt she shouldn't broach the subject now. She was sure he would rather not house the children of her previous marriage under his roof. He would likely want her to focus on any children they might have together.

But that was being unfair to him. She would ask him, but later. When the time felt right.

"What a pleasant evening," Thomas said as they stepped back onto the waiting barge. "I don't know what I expected, but it wasn't that." He held out a hand for Elizabeth, who gladly accepted.

"Things went smoothly," she said by way of agreeing.

Thomas snickered, a sly smile going over her head to Edward behind her.

"What?"

"The two of you seemed rather...talkative."

"Should I not be talking to my betrothed? We are to be married in less than two months."

The barge creaked as Edward stepped on board, nodding to the helmsman to set off. "Yes, dearest sister, it was all well and good, but now we must question how many other times the two of you may have talked. You seemed like you were quite good friends. It is untoward."

"Seriously, Edward. I find it hard to take a rebuke from you now. I have done as the family wished and am agreeing to marry, though I would have preferred to die an old widow."

"A poor one," Thomas chimed in.

Edward rewarded him with a look, but Elizabeth crossed her arms in front of her. "I shouldn't be if my family would look after me properly."

"I think she is accusing us, Edward." Thomas was frowning.

"Merely teasing. I do not wish to be a charity case, but all things considered, I could hardly be poor with my two wonderful brothers looking out for me."

Edward shook his head, as though not wishing to argue about this further.

The river was quiet as they rowed back upriver to the palace. Lanterns lit their way, but the boatmen seemed to be able to see in the dark. Elizabeth sat on a chair, listening to the sound of the water lapping gently against the side of the barge. Above, the full moon shone brightly. It had been a pleasant night indeed.

She crept into her bed after sharing a cup of hot wine with her brothers, demanding they go over the details of her marriage contract with her. Even though she liked Gregory well enough, she wanted to make sure she was being well provided for, and she did not like to remain ignorant on such matters.

She retreated to her room.

Elizabeth tried to be quiet when she climbed into bed, but Madge still woke up. "You were out late."

"I was with my brothers."

"Hmm, your sister was asking for you, but it was Lady Rochford who ended up going to her," Madge said between yawns. "The king did not visit tonight."

Elizabeth stood up. "Should I see if she needs me?"

"It was nothing, I am sure. She knew you were gone somewhere. Don't be concerned." Madge was more awake now, alert, as though watching her.

"I am not concerned. I am sorry to not have been here to help my sister though," Elizabeth said. Forcing herself to be calmer, she tucked herself under the warm blankets. The fire had died down a long time ago and the room had become chilly. She sighed in satisfaction as she laid her head down. "Good night, Madge. Thank you for informing me."

"Good night."

Elizabeth listened as the woman settled back down to sleep. She was watching the shadows play on the ceiling. Outside, the wind had picked up and the trees swayed, causing shadows in her room.

She tried to sleep. Tried not to worry over her sister. Rushing to her rooms would make matters worse. She said a silent prayer and counted the weeks remaining until her sister would deliver. Then, hopefully, they would be safe and happy and not have to watch their every move and step.

Not for the first time, she found herself wishing herself far away from court.

The countryside had its own share of problems, but there wasn't this fear and anxiety, at least not for her.

She hadn't thought to ask Gregory where they would settle down. Would he still wish for them to be at court often? She hoped not. It would be a good excuse to escape.

There were so many things they still had to ask each other.

She couldn't believe that soon she'd be led down the aisle yet again.

CHAPTER SIX

"You may pick anything out of my wardrobe," Jane said graciously, a hand resting on her belly, a habit she had developed shortly after confirming she was with child. It was still hard to tell, but her sister had found that her gowns had become tight and new panels would have to be added once loosening the laces was no longer enough.

In the evenings, as she prepared for bed, the thin nightshift made her condition more obvious. Her belly was curved, a sure sign a child was growing there. There had been a few stressful weeks as the whole court waited for the child to quicken. It had made Jane quick-tempered. Once she had felt the baby move, Jane regained her calm composure.

"I do like this blue gown," Elizabeth said, fingering the soft silk between her fingertips. It was a light-blue silk, probably from Italy. The sleeves were etched with copious amounts of white lace. Elizabeth had the feeling it would look splendid without being over the top.

"You are sure you would not like my velvets?"

Elizabeth laughed. "That would not be appropriate, Your Grace. They would be much too fine for me." She didn't want to give people the wrong impression and dress above her station. As a lady-in-waiting she was technically exempt from the sumptuary laws that governed how someone could dress. However, there were enough rumours going around court about how the Cromwells were reaching far above their station. She did not want to add more fuel to the fire.

Jane blinked and then, as though she pieced it together herself, nodded. "Silly of me. I forget, why are you marrying him? I thought our brother could get you an earl at least."

Elizabeth gave her a thin smile. "We can't all have your luck, sister. I am lucky to have even gotten him."

Jane pursed her lips but dropped the subject as the other ladies reappeared, carrying in trunks of goods. The queen's jewels.

Jane sifted through the collection before settling upon a pair of fine diamond earrings.

"These would suit you," she said, handing them over to her.

"Your Grace, I don't..."

"Just to wear on your wedding day," Jane said, turning to Lady Rochford nearby. "Make a note of that somewhere. You may borrow them from the royal treasury for one day."

Elizabeth dipped her sister a low respectful curtsy. "Thank you for your generosity."

She couldn't say no now, could she? It wasn't that she didn't appreciate the gesture, but she had no need for these diamonds. She supposed this was her sister's way of sharing the wealth, but it was misguided. If only her sister had the influence to give her what she wanted: her children and independence.

She imagined Jane was trying to make up for her first wedding, which had been a very private affair and her family had not afforded her such luxuries then. Nor did her husband shower her with expensive gifts and presents. She had always been the younger daughter of an unimportant family, until the scandal with her father had made them known to all of England.

⁓

The day had arrived. It did not seem to matter that it was overcast. She would be allowed to get married in the queen's chapel, the very place her sister had said her vows months prior.

She bathed and dressed in that pale blue dress, allowing a maid to pin her hair back. There were no bawdy jests for her this morning, and thankfully no embarrassing conversation with her mother.

It would have felt like any other day. Except after this morning, she would no longer be Lady Ughtred but become Lady Cromwell.

It was all very simply done.

Her brother, as head of the family, was the one who escorted her to the chapel door where the priest waited with her groom. Gregory looked handsome in what seemed to be a new dark-grey suit. The slashes on his sleeves revealed a cream-coloured shirt peeking through. His hair had recently been clipped short like the king's. It did not suit him well, but neither did the gable hood suit her sister. It was the king who set the fashion, not them.

She surprised herself by how calm she felt as she took her place by his side. With one glance at each other they turned as one toward the priest, who began by asking them if there was any reason that they knew of that would prevent them from marrying. They both answered with no.

"Do you both consent to taking each other in holy matrimony?" he asked, his tone monotone.

"I do," Elizabeth said, after forgetting that simply nodding wouldn't be enough.

The rings were placed on the Bible and the priest said a prayer in Latin. The church was reformed, but many of its old customs were retained. They exchanged rings. She was surprised by how heavy her gold band felt on her finger. Gregory gave her a quick smile. Then the priest blessed them, declaring them man and wife before turning and leading them into the chapel. The witnesses, their family members, marching in behind them. The priest recited his psalm and then held a mass.

They knelt before him as a veil was thrown over them, covering them from sight. Gregory gave her a wink and she smiled in return. It felt all very silly. She wasn't some blushing bride nor overly religious, so she didn't take this to heart and she was eager to be able to stand again.

Finally, the priest finished and the veil was removed. They stood as man and wife. It was done. The families' fortunes were now interlocked together.

Elizabeth was fortunate on many accounts that no fuss was made over this wedding, as there was no public bedding ceremony.

They broke their fast together as a new family, with hired performers and a fool who took to juggling the Spanish oranges served at the table. A few bawdy jokes were made but nothing to cause a scene. It was a very civil way to spend the morning. She even received her sister's congratulations and the king said a kind word to her, though he did not stay for the whole celebration.

They were rowed downriver to Austin Friars to spend their first wedding night together away from court.

Now her courage had left her somewhat. Gregory, as nice as he was, was still little more than a stranger.

They didn't speak on the whole trek. Thomas Cromwell, the Lord Privy Seal, was accompanying them. He was like a dark shadow over the proceedings. She knew she shouldn't fear him. He had done nothing to her, but there was something off-putting about him. Something that told her she wanted to avoid being around him for long. Just looking at him you felt like you could be in danger.

Perhaps it was this that kept the silence on the barge.

When they arrived at Austin Friars, torches had been

lit all the way up the path, and she appreciated how happy they all seemed to be that the young Master Cromwell was married at last.

They peppered her with fresh flowers and songs.

Wine had been flowing freely all morning.

At the doorway, Cromwell turned to the pair of them and beckoned forth a waiting servant carrying a large chest.

"For you, a gift on the day of your wedding. From now on you won't have to wear hand-me-downs from your relations," he said with some sincere generosity.

Elizabeth blushed. She had not realized that perhaps he would recognize the dress or the jewels she wore, but of course he would. He was renowned for knowing everything. Nothing was too small or unimportant for his attention.

Cromwell flung the lid open to reveal a wealth of beautiful cloth to be made into a new gown for her. On top of this rich material was a necklace of sapphires, each the size of her thumbnail, with earrings to match.

She gaped, unsure what to say.

"You are too generous," she said with a curtsy.

"It has been a long time since there was a lady of the house," he said with a smile. "You will find I am happy to spoil those of my household. Just ask my son."

Gregory's smile was tight, but he did not seem too put out.

She was shown around, this time being given a more extensive tour before being shown to her bedchamber. The room was decorated with garlands of greenery and fresh flowers, filling the air with a sweet scent. She really felt like a bride now.

Two maids came in to help her get changed, and she slipped into a warm furred robe for the evening as she waited for her new husband to join her.

She waited for quite some time by the fireside, watching the logs burn up and nearly die into glowing embers before there was a tap at her door.

"Come in," she called out, and in he stepped with an apologetic look as he bowed to her.

"I was getting worried I would be spending our first night together alone. Imagine the scandal of being rejected."

She saw the pearly whites of his teeth as his lips twisted into that now familiar grin. He stepped closer still and she could see he had brought a decanter of wine.

"Did you forget the glasses?"

"I did," he said. "But I won't tell if you don't." He offered her the bottle.

Her eyebrow arched, but she took him up on it. She took a swig, unused to drinking from a bottle, and sputtered a bit.

He laughed. "Ah, you have married among the common folk. You will get used to it."

"Nothing about this feels common," she said with a shrug, indicating her robe, lined with the softest marten fur she had felt. She thought of the jewels she had been presented with. Those were worth a fortune, but she knew it wasn't for her that they were given but rather the Cromwell name.

They were building a new dynasty. They didn't have the ancestry, but they had the money and they would flaunt it so people would take them seriously.

"Was this all you ever hoped for?"

She gave a smile. "I have no expectations." She took another swig off the bottle before offering it back to him. "Well, perhaps that is not true," she said, licking the remainder of the wine off her lips. She caught him watching the movement. "I suppose if I had a wish it would be that you turn out to be a kind husband to me and loyal. I suspect you shall be though."

He took a swig too. "I will work day and night for your approval."

"My valiant knight." She leaned forward, kissing him. Tasting the wine on his lips.

"I haven't been knighted yet," he said, but his words sounded far away. She thought she could hear the desire in his voice, now awakened.

She rested back on her chair, a knowing smile on her lips.

"I am sure your father would deny you nothing."

"I would really rather not talk about my father right now." He stood, holding out his hand to her. An inviting look.

She smiled, placing her hand in his. It felt right. He made her feel safe and secure. She supposed it was because she saw the good man hiding behind his courtly facade. A rarity, given his upbringing and lineage.

"Shall we go to bed, husband?" she said as he pulled her to her feet after he had set down the wine bottle.

"Yes, I do like the sound of that," he said before surprising her by lifting her off the ground. Literally sweeping her off her feet, and she found herself in his arms being carried to their bed.

"I don't remember agreeing to being carried." She pouted.

"Hush now." He silenced her with a kiss before letting her fall on the bed.

"It's a good thing you didn't have far to go. This robe weighs more than me. I can assume this was not easy on you," she said, for she had felt him falter once or twice. "I should have had you carry me across the threshold as would be proper to truly prove your strength."

His eyes seemed to twinkle mischievously in the candlelight. "Perhaps I should start by removing this offending robe, then."

She laughed, but her heart started beating faster. She seemed to dare him to do it. He was beside her in the next moment, a hand snaking behind her head as he tilted her head up to meet his kiss. This one was not as chaste as the last had been. She felt her own desire mounting.

It felt good to have a man in her bed once more.

∽

She would not be away from court for long. They still had their duties to attend to and would not be released from them until Parliament dissolved.

Gregory would be sent to the country with her this

summer to take possession of the estate his father had purchased there and take his seat in the Parliament.

"Will you be displeased to leave London?" he asked the next morning, trailing kisses from her neck to her shoulder.

She shuddered but shook her head. "No, I must return to be with my sister when she goes into her confinement, but I am not sad to leave court. I cannot do much for my sister here, but I have done much for the family in marrying you."

He looked indignant at the insult, but she saw how his lips kept twitching to break into a smile.

She turned herself around, hair falling loosely down her back. "I am being serious, but that does not mean I don't like you or that you should feel insulted. Most marriages are merely arrangements. But if you want, I could try to play the part of the lovesick fool."

He seemed to consider her suggestion quite seriously. "As amusing as that would be, I think it would be best to leave it as you said. Though I hope you enjoyed our time together."

She nodded.

"I know my father was keen to see me married for quite some time. He wants to ensure I do my duty by this family and continue the family line."

She blushed scarlet at the thought of her father-in-law searching high and low for a fertile wife for his son.

"I did not know he was so enthusiastic about that."

"Oh, I am sure he would have been happy to see me married to a laundry maid."

"Is that all I am? Or just slightly better because I come from a good family?"

"I forget that you cannot take insults as well as you hand them out." He moved off the bed, planting a kiss on her brow. "I wasn't willing to just marry anyone my father threw at me. But he likes you and thinks this is a good match."

She nodded, appeased, but she slipped on her robe again, playing with the ties around her waist. He had raised the topic of children; now would be an opportune moment to mention her own. She looked up to find he was slipping on his clothing, humming a light tune.

She would wait. When they had a few more carefree days together, then she would broach the subject.

∼

Her plans to slip back into the queen's chamber without being noticed were thwarted by her own sister.

"Good morning, Lady Cromwell. I hope the trip by barge wasn't too cumbersome."

Elizabeth winced at the chuckles and snorts of laughter that sprang from the ladies.

Jane looked around, not sure why they were laughing.

"The river was quiet, though it was a chilly day, but thank you, Your Grace," Elizabeth said with a polite curtsy.

She had to remind herself several times that day to keep her calm. People liked to gossip and bored ladies-in-waiting were no better. Besides, this was the first piece of good news that they had heard for quite some time. It was annoying to always be worrying about rebellions and princesses imprisoned in towers. It was much easier and more fun to tease a newly married woman.

Unfortunately for them, there was nothing for her to say. She was glad that this was not her first marriage, that she had a good head on her shoulders. Nor did she want to share her delight in the marriage bed. That had been a surprise to her as well.

With her previous husband, everything had been done for the sake of duty. She loved her children greatly, but the act itself was a mere formality. At least he had also been kind and considerate. She knew that wasn't always the case.

The queen's condition precluded her from joining the king on most of his outings. She dared not ride or excite herself too much. Henry seemed to have the same idea, but he did not wish to limit himself to the company of his gentlemen and attendants. Many ladies were invited to go with him on his excursions, and Elizabeth was among them.

"Ah, the lovely bride," the king said when he saw her striding into the courtyard, dressed in a new riding gown of dark green. The colour was so deep it looked almost black. He seemed to frown at her and turned a teasing smile to Gregory, who stood off to the side.

"I see you have dressed her in the colours of your new family," he said in a tone of mock seriousness. "It doesn't suit her so well."

"It was not my intention, Your Majesty," Gregory said, springing forward.

"I like it, Your Majesty," Elizabeth interjected boldly. "I feel like a clerk. Maybe in this way I will have my husband's attention more."

A laugh. Her bawdy jest struck the right chord between what was proper and improper.

The courtiers behind them laughed as well.

Gregory stepped forward to kiss her hand and help her mount her horse.

"See how the young master takes care of his wife. He will put us all to shame," the king said, a hand to his great belly. "Well, let us hope we shall be just as successful on our own hunt today."

They cheered.

She rode by Gregory's side, sharing titbits of her morning with him and asking how he did.

"You really didn't have to wear such a dark dress," he said, clearly embarrassed.

"The dress was meant to be green, but clearly there must have been a mistake at the dyers. But I do like it. I feel very sophisticated."

"You look more like a widow," he said, a slight frown as he looked at her.

"I am in mourning for my freedom then, for I have woken this morning to find it was whisked away."

This got a chuckle out of him.

"Very well, but I wouldn't want people to think you are miserable."

"I hardly doubt a miserable woman would have joined her husband and much less ridden beside him."

He seemed to consider her. The very little distance they seemed to be keeping between them. How people who looked their way seemed to have a secret smile on their lips.

"Well, I suppose I am a fool, for I am the last to know you are happy."

"Not a fool by any means. I wouldn't tolerate such a husband," she said. She wanted to say more, but the trumpets began blowing. The dogs had found their quarry.

"Let's go," she said, urging her horse forward. The whole party began riding hard. The wind whipped at her face, bringing colour into her cheeks. She thought about what she had said. She supposed she was somewhat lighter of spirit.

Could she dare hope to be happy in this new marriage with such an unlikely candidate?

∽

A month went by and they settled into a routine. She would join him in their rooms on most nights and they would enjoy the freedoms marriage permitted them. Once he took her out on a small picnic, just the pair of them.

It was a lazy time. The country was at peace. The queen's belly was growing. Lady Margaret Douglas was moved to Syon Abbey, so there was hope she would be pardoned eventually. All was well.

Then, as summer approached and she was beginning to prepare to leave to see her husband's home, she realized something that shook her to her core.

She had been foolish and lazy and not keeping track of the time, but it had been weeks since she had last bled. She bit her nail, trying to recall the last time she had asked her maid for napkins.

It was shortly after her wedding. That was over a month and a half ago. She cursed her fertility, but it was too soon to tell for sure.

She wouldn't say anything to anyone, not yet.

How would it look that her sister had struggled so long to get pregnant when she, barely married a month, might have conceived a child already? She sighed. The king might not take it kindly to have the comparison made. There would be no winning. The blame would be laid at her sister's door or her husband's for daring to show up the king in such a way.

She would have to speak to her father-in-law about how to best proceed. He seemed to know how to best manage the king.

A week later and the tell-tale sign of feeling ill throughout the day confirmed her suspicions.

It made it harder to conceal. Certain scents made her want to run for the chamber pot. When the early roses bloomed and the ladies walked through the garden to enjoy them, she fought to keep down the bile rising in her throat.

"You seem to be developing the Cromwell scowl. I had not known it was catching," Jane Rochford said on one such morning, sidling up beside her.

Elizabeth looked at her. "Whatever do you mean?"

Jane grinned. "Do you not know what you look like? No wonder you've been keeping to your sister's chambers the last few days. Have you scared off your husband with your frowns?"

"She needed me the last few nights."

"Oh?" Jane looked intrigued. "Is there something wrong?"

"No, of course not. Her feet are sore, that is all. A common occurrence during pregnancy, and she's been needing to use the chamber pot a lot."

"Of course." Jane nodded, though she did not seem to buy it.

Perhaps it would have been easier to let her believe that it was marital problems with her husband that were causing her to sleep in her sister's rooms.

At least Jane did not seem too suspicious. Perhaps she didn't think that her husband would wish to lie with her. After all, Jane's husband had been disinclined to do so, and if rumours were to be believed, he preferred his sister's company to hers.

Looking at the sour-faced Jane, always ready with a rude word, it wasn't hard to believe.

It was getting harder to avoid Gregory though, and she did not wish to outright lie to him.

When he pressed her as to why she was avoiding their bed and his company, she had tried waving him off.

"I am not avoiding you, but my duties are keeping me occupied."

"Your sister does well enough without you," Gregory said, starting to seem puzzled. "Is the honeymoon over so soon?"

She nearly choked on her own words. He didn't know the half of it.

Now was not the time to say anything though. They were in a crowded arena watching a tennis match playing out. It would be impossible to have a private word with him here. Even more so, not the way she wanted to tell him.

"I'll come to you tonight, I promise." She gave him a peck on his cheek to placate him.

It worked, and he wrapped his arms around her waist, pulling her close. The smell of horse and his cologne mingled together, causing her to have another bout of nausea that she had to hold down.

If he was hurt that she ran out of his arms as soon as the match was over, he didn't show it, but she suspected he was suspicious and she would have some explaining to do tonight.

The fireplace had been stoked high and the heat emanating from it was starting to make her sweat. She had her maid undress her and help her plait her hair in a braid.

The tension in her head eased as the comb ran

through her hair.

"You've been tired, milady," her maid commented. "Shall I ask for a doctor to come see you? Perhaps some medicine would help you."

She shook her head. "No, I will be fine. Some rest will do wonders."

She doubted the potions doctors concocted could do much for her. Just as she had seen the trickeries that took place at holy shrines, of statues crying blood, she doubted that those mixtures contained anything that could actually help her. The times she had taken something for a cold or headache she had felt worse.

"Thank you for your concern. Soon I'll be in the country, and the fresh air will do me good." She wanted to be kind to her.

Not long after she was cleaned up and ready for bed, in fact, yearning to climb under the warm covers and lay her head down on the soft pillows, Gregory snuck in. He was quiet, much like he had been on that first night they spent together. But this time he looked ready for a fight, or at the very least some long debate.

She looked at him with a questioning glance as he began pacing the room.

"I want to speak before you go ahead and give yourself a heart attack," Elizabeth said as though she was talking to an irritated child.

He opened his mouth to say something, but she silenced him with one look.

"Yes, I admit I have been avoiding you, but it is not because of what you might think. I assume you are not displeased with me, and I am not displeased with you. That being said, I do have news that will cause a few bumps." She couldn't help but laugh at her own little joke. "I wanted to wait to be sure before I spring the news on everyone. You are the first to know."

He looked at her, quite confused now.

"What are you trying to say?"

Elizabeth took a deep breath, tucking a strand of hair behind her ear. "I'm with child. Yours if you must know."

He looked taken aback, but then a brilliant smile spread across his face, illuminating even his eyes. "Are you sure?"

"All the signs are there," she said, a smile on her own face. His happiness was infectious.

"Then what is the problem?" But even as he asked the question it dawned on him. "We cannot worry about that now. We shall hide you away in the country until we are sure. There's no point upsetting anyone. I am so happy." He rushed over and took her in his arms.

Elizabeth sighed contentedly in his tight embrace.

Then he froze and pulled away. "Was I harming the baby? I am sorry."

"No, it felt good. I have been feeling the stress hiding this away from everyone. It feels better to tell someone else," she said.

He kissed her on the lips. "I cannot wait to shout it from the rooftops that I am to have a child."

She gave him a sly look. "You men are all the same. So boastful when really it is us women that do most of the work."

Gregory scoffed but held her again. "We shall have to tell my father. If he doesn't know already. Then we will try to plan for our move to the country."

"Sounds perfect." She rested her head against his chest. "I just want to rest. And perhaps we can see my children too?"

She finally asked.

He nodded. "We will plan something. Don't worry."

Thomas Cromwell stood a little straighter as they told him their news, but he was not displeased. He looked at her with something akin to admiration and congratulated his son.

"It will be nice to have a little one crawling around here again," he said when all the traditional things were said. "Gregory used to hide among my papers as a little boy, barely walking. He always caused such a mess."

Elizabeth laughed, not being able to imagine her neat husband causing such havoc.

"It's true the nursemaids didn't know what to do with me, but my father told them to let me be and said that he would put me to work."

"And did he?" she asked, looking between the two men. This was a rare instance for her to witness their familial bond.

"Oh yes, he would give me little notes to run up and down to either the cook or my mother. I'm sure they were nonsense, but I felt like I was doing something important.

Sometimes I would get distracted on my way back, so he was saved from me for a time."

"That was a clever trick," Elizabeth said with a grin. "I'll have to keep it in mind."

"Going back to the matter at hand, I think it would be a good thing to keep the news restricted to those close to the family. There's no point boasting about it around court. Are we in agreement about that?" Lord Cromwell said.

Elizabeth nodded, as did her husband.

"How do you think he will take the news?"

"Depends on the day, but let the queen, your sister's belly grow larger and he will become content enough to let others start their own families as well," Lord Cromwell replied to his son's inquiry.

She couldn't help but snort with laughter. "It really is silly."

He fixed her with that dark gaze and she froze, shutting her mouth tight.

"I meant to say that..." She was at a loss for words, so she merely shrugged. "Well, I won't tell my sister, as I don't want her to worry about the comparison, but I might tell my brother Edward. He will keep my secret."

Thomas Cromwell seemed to consider and then nodded.

"If you think he can be trusted."

"With this, yes," she said without hesitation. She wasn't a fool. She knew from experience that not everything would keep her brother quiet, but he had nothing to gain by blabbing this around court.

"Then the pair of you are dismissed with my congratulations."

Thomas Cromwell was already pulling dossiers toward him, ready to take care of stately business.

Gregory helped her to her feet as though she was already heavy with child. She let him dote on her, finding it sweet of him to care for her so much already. There was many a man who did not care one bit whether or not his wife was with a child. She had seen it herself how many women had to go out to work in the fields despite their great bellies. She'd heard that many gave birth in those fields and then went back about their work. She said a silent prayer, thanking God she was more fortunate. She had been through enough births to know that it wasn't so easy, even when one was attended by a gaggle of midwives and serving women.

∽

They travelled south as slowly as they could manage.

Gregory was insistent she take care and ride in a litter. She was only two months along at most, and she would likely not have known it herself if this had been her first pregnancy. She tried to tell him that this would likely draw attention, but he had been deaf to her concerns.

After a day and a half of being pestered by black flies and mosquitos at sunset, Elizabeth begged him to quicken their pace.

"I promise you I am not a fragile flower. I know

myself well enough by now to know how to take care of myself. But these flies"—she showed him the welts on her arms and the bites on her neck— "will be the death of me. So please let's quicken our pace."

He scratched his own bites. "It is awful traveling in summer."

She nodded. At least it was more manageable not traveling through such marshy lands and lakes.

At last he relented and they quickened their pace. Their guards and servants seemed especially grateful to her after that and always seemed to take special care of her and give her preference over him.

Finally, they arrived. Elizabeth hung out of the litter to get a better view of the manor home. It was a great building. It had been built new from old stone recovered from an abbey nearby on the ruins of an old castle. The wall had been torn down, but she could still make out where it would have stood by the harsh lines cutting around the manor.

They rode past a well-stocked fishpond and an orchard.

Leave it to Cromwell to ensure every inch of his land was productive.

"My father enjoys beautiful things, but I think he prefers it when he can turn them around to sell," Gregory said, guessing at her thoughts.

"He's a smart man. Prudent."

"Is that a compliment?"

She stuck out her tongue, a very unladylike gesture that made him chuckle.

"I am glad you are not like the other women at court. They are too prim and proper. They would have placed high expectations on me already. You have hardly asked for anything since we've been married," he said wistfully.

"You married a wild country girl without knowing it," she shot back to him. A mischievous grin on her face, but she pulled away from the opening to lean against the cushions. He was not entirely correct. She had not asked because the one thing she wanted…she wasn't sure how to ask. Perhaps she was afraid of what he would say or of not being able to. That it would close the final door on her hopes of having her children back in her keeping.

She rubbed a hand over her belly, where a new child was growing. It felt wrong that a child could be taken away from a mother like that. After all, the child was a part of her. It was the mother who gave them life. Why were men given dominion over all?

She shook her head to clear her thoughts. There was no point wondering about how unfair the world was.

"We are almost there," Gregory's voice called out. "I'll ride ahead to make sure they are ready for us."

She doubted they were unprepared. Their retinue had been kicking up a cloud of dust all the way from London. It had been a dry summer and it only made it worse.

They passed through the gatehouse, which still stood, the Cromwell arms freshly carved into stone.

It was a large intimidating building up close. A suitable seat of power for an aspiring lord. She was happy to note the large stables. There would be plenty of opportunities for her to go riding once she was able.

Her eyes landed on the main building at last. It had been freshly plastered and seemed to almost sparkle in the summer sun.

It seemed like most of the household members had come out to greet them.

She watched as Gregory jumped down with an easy grace from his horse, his hand held up in greeting, calling many people by their names.

He seemed at ease among these people. There wasn't the sort of formality of court life.

The litter finally came to a stop and he ran over, helping her down himself.

Pulling her around, he introduced her to the steward, the chamberlain, and his secretary. She was used to seeing a lot of people and greeting them all by now, but she was still taken aback by the exuberance they showed her.

"I have never seen such happy people," she commented to Gregory as he led her inside.

"We aren't serious folk. We are easy with each other. Perhaps we break a few rules that we shouldn't."

When she looked at him questioningly, he explained. "Oftentimes we don't observe the order of rank as strictly as you would expect. One summer my father himself climbed up on the roof to inspect the tiles. But that's a secret that doesn't leave this house."

Elizabeth laughed. "You are right. I cannot believe it.

And don't worry, your secret's safe with me. Even if I did share it, no one would believe it."

"Let me show you the house and your rooms," he said, pulling her inside. "You shall have your work cut out for you decorating some of them. We bought this house without any furnishings, so only the bare bones are here."

"Shall we not have a bed to sleep in?" she asked, trying to judge how bad matters had gotten.

"We shall have to bed down with the animals in the straw."

She swatted at his arm, knowing he was teasing. "If that were true, you would see me jump on a horse and ride back to London right now. Baby or no baby."

They stepped inside and Elizabeth could see what he meant. The corridors were empty and felt eerie. The dining hall held a large table and a few chairs here and there.

A lot would have to be brought in if they were ever going to entertain people of note here. She could never imagine having the king and queen staying with them.

He took her up to the west wing. He kept looking back at her with a knowing smile on his lips.

"Why do you keep looking at me like that?"

"Like what?"

"Like you know something I don't."

He shrugged.

Elizabeth pursed her lips and wanted to tell him that more than anything she desired a bath and a bed to rest in after the long journey.

"Steady yourself," he said as they turned a corner.

"For what?"

"Patience," he said, giving her hand a squeeze before nodding to a pair of page boys waiting by double doors.

They threw the doors open and Gregory rushed her inside.

"Mama!"

Elizabeth was in shock at the scene before her.

Little Henry stood up from playing with a set of toy soldiers. His nurses were already standing at attention. While a third let little Margery toddle over to her.

Elizabeth turned to Gregory with her mouth gaping. "Am I dreaming? What are they doing here?"

She dropped all decorum and fell to her knees, allowing Henry to come embrace her in a hug.

First he had looked to his nursemaids and bowed too, then flung his scrawny arms around her.

She was weeping. Gregory placed a hand on her shoulder as she wiped her tears away.

"I had not expected to see them here. How long are they to stay? What a wonderful surprise!" She rushed over to Margery and threw her up in the air before squeezing her tight. Her heart was leaping with happiness.

"Maybe I shouldn't have surprised you like this." He was grinning, and she caught the wetness in his own eyes.

"Are you crying, milord?" she asked in a whisper.

"It is true I am a sensitive man. I cannot help but see your joy and think of our own growing family and the way things were for my family before my mother and sisters passed away. I am happy to have made you so happy," he admitted.

She licked her lips, finding them dry. "I still cannot believe it. Words cannot describe how happy I am."

She was on her knees again, hugging and playing with her children.

"I haven't even told you the best part yet. They are to stay and live with us."

"What? Really? Wait, say it again." She was gaping like a simpleton.

"They are to live with us. I have purchased their wardship away from their grandfather."

"You did that for me?"

"Yes. If it helps to think of me as a mean old grouch, then know that it was a good financial decision on my part too."

She grinned. "I am sure it was."

"Young Henry here shall have to go visiting his grandfather, and we have agreed that he shall be fostered among his family once it is time for him to be educated. Unless we can find somewhere better."

"Oh, that is lovely. Did you hear that, Henry? We shall not be parted again."

The little boy smiled but seemed not to understand the gravity of it. It hurt her a bit, but she supposed it was not surprising given how little time they had spent together of late.

"Mama, you promised I might have a horse when I am big enough. Am I big enough now?" he asked with large doe-like eyes.

Gregory laughed. "I see now how hard it is to not give children their every desire." He patted Henry on the head. Henry did not really appreciate the gesture but didn't shrug him off either.

"I'll tell you what, Henry, I will let you ride in the saddle with me, and then when your new stepfather here thinks you are ready he shall find you a pony of your very own," she said, smoothly passing responsibility over to Gregory.

He grimaced, having been tricked into being made responsible for this.

"Shall I always be the one to say no? Is it not enough that I brought them here for you?"

She grinned up at him, though winced when Margery tugged at the chain around her neck.

"You shall have your practice with them. You may find it hard to harden your heart to your own child even more."

Henry looked between the two of them as though trying to solve a puzzle.

"You are my father now?" he asked.

"Stepfather," Gregory corrected.

Henry seemed to be deep in thought. "Will you die too?"

Both Gregory and Elizabeth let out a gasp.

"I certainly hope not. I plan to be around for many more years to come. I have proven to your mother I am quite useful, and I doubt she will let me go all that soon."

Every adult in the room chuckled, and that made little Maggie let out a laugh of her own.

"Very well, sir," Henry said, with all the seriousness of a barrister passing judgment.

"Are you pleased, Henry?" Elizabeth asked.

"I am," came the little reply.

Elizabeth bit her lip to keep from laughing again; he seemed to have taken it badly the first time.

"Shall I leave you here, then? I have some matters to attend to."

Elizabeth nodded. "But if it's any more surprises, please know I cannot handle any more at this time.

"Oh sweetheart, if only I could have had a painter sketch your face when you saw your children. That expression is burned into my mind forever. I don't think I shall ever be able to make you replicate it."

He looked like he wanted to kiss her but did not do so in front of the children. With an exaggerated bow, he swept them a curtsy and left.

The first weeks at Oakham Hall were bliss for Elizabeth.

She had all she could ever want and enjoyed chasing Henry around the empty rooms while a scribe followed after them trying to make a list of all the things she wanted for each of the rooms.

Margery was still too young to play such games, but Elizabeth played with her as much as possible too.

They painted a lovely picture of a picturesque country family. It reminded Elizabeth of the old days at Wolf Hall when she was still just a child.

Edward wrote to her once or twice to see how she was doing and give her news that her sister continued to thrive. Elizabeth was interested in hearing more than this, but Edward was hardly likely to commit gossip to paper.

As this was her third child, her belly began showing faster than Jane's had. Her laces could no longer be tightened properly, so there was little chance of hiding it when they returned to court.

She had agreed to go into confinement with Jane when her time came in September, so it would have been impossible to keep it from her.

She urged Gregory to write to tell his father that it would soon be time to let their secret out.

She had to admire how much Gregory was trying to take care of her. He marvelled at her growing belly and loved feeling the child stir in her womb. It felt strong, from the little kicks it was already giving her. She must be in her fourth month by now. A honeymoon baby.

Their time in this little paradise was coming to an end.

She desperately didn't want it to, but there was nothing for it.

Elizabeth was greeted with a lengthy letter from her sister one morning, and she knew that the end was near.

Her sister wrote to congratulate her and said that the king was excited that his son should have a little cousin the same age to play with in the nursery. Then she went on to say how she missed her company and couldn't wait to see her at court.

She had adjusted quickly to being back in the country. She supposed it shouldn't have surprised her, but now that the very real prospect of heading back to court was upon her she wasn't sure how to feel. At least the worst was out of the way and everyone knew she was with child. If there had been any blowback, she hadn't been there to witness it.

They packed up to leave for court, but Elizabeth refused to let her children remain behind.

"You cannot expect me to be separated from them now after all this time, can you?" She was holding on to Maggie's little hands as she tried to catch up to her brother with unsteady steps.

Gregory looked uncertain.

"I don't know if the court is the best place for children."

"But of course it is. Besides, soon my sister will give birth and the little prince will need playmates," she said with a smile.

"You are making one for him now," he said, a hand to her belly. "I just don't want you straining yourself."

"I promise you I would be more worried about them if I left them behind. If they are with me, I will sleep easy."

"If you say so, my love," Gregory said, pulling away.

"I love how I know when you are humouring me. You always call me 'my love.' Never gamble, my lord. You could never keep a straight face."

He laughed. "Not around you, that's for sure. But don't forget you have had the privilege of knowing me."

She elbowed him in the side. "Your teasing infuriates me."

"I recall I had infuriated you a lot on the night you must have conceived this little one. Look how he grows. How big will you get before it is your time?"

"Hopefully smaller than the doorway or I will have to have you expand the doorways. That would prove costly indeed."

He nodded, a grave expression on his face. "I am sure my father would find a way. He's good at squeezing money from a rock."

"Such a way with words."

∽

As the family packed up to leave, the workmen moved in. A large patch of forest would be cleared away, and the roof was leaking in some parts of the house. All this work would be done while they were away, and hopefully they would come back to the fixed-up house.

They were also to tear down the wood panelling and paint fresh frescos on the walls. The carpenter would also repaint the dark timber beams.

It would be a beautiful house when it was finished, with plenty of room for them all.

The children were excited by the novelty of traveling on the road. It was hard to keep them still in the litter, and Elizabeth could see Gregory laughing behind her back at her struggling to wrangle her wildlings.

At length she discovered that letting them run

around in the grassy meadows whenever possible was excellent for tiring them out. Initially, she had been scared they might get hurt, but they needed some way to burn off some of that energy. Then when they came across a bramble of berry bushes, she took them on an excursion to pick as many as they could.

They fell asleep with their heads on her lap, their clothes stained in places with the juices of the berries. She didn't mind but sighed contentedly and rested her head back to drift off to sleep. She would worry about the cost of fabric and new clothes another time.

~

London's dusty streets were full of people coming and going.

Elizabeth pulled back the covers of the litter for her children to see. As they passed by a group of hungry beggars, she threw a few coins to the downtrodden. Why did it seem to her like they were looking more out of sorts than usual? The summer had been dry and the harvest would not be as good as usual, but at least it would not be a failed harvest like in other years.

The king's changes were constant, and people were living in constant fear of being turned out of doors. Monasteries that used to take care of the poor were no longer open. Many had been closed, with their treasures going into the king's own treasury, but he had not been as generous as the monks.

Elizabeth did not deny that many of the monks and

priests were corrupt, taking a fortune from people in order to provide them with blessings, but at the same time they had done some charitable works.

To her it seemed that the king was squandering and hoarding his new wealth. He wanted to fund a war with France. He didn't want to worry himself over the welfare of these unimportant citizens.

Elizabeth looked at Gregory, who was riding, his back straight as a board, through the town. She had asked him once why his father did not suggest some way to remedy the poverty that seemed to be growing in England, but he had remained silent.

"My father is generous. I know he does not seem like it, but you must remember he holds a lot of contempt for the nobility. He came from those streets, practically a beggar himself. He tries to be kind."

"He also hoards wealth. I have not seen him opening his kitchens to these hungry folk," she had said, unable to keep herself from accusing him.

Gregory had sighed. "It is not as easy as that. Trust me when I say he helps when he can. He always takes on more clerks and workers than he needs in order to offer more people a living wage. He has been supporting the king's colleges out of his own pocket because he knows how important education is. He is not tight-fisted. He has been very generous with you."

Elizabeth had blushed, looking down at her hands in her lap. It was true she was making accusations when she herself had benefited from this. Not only that, but she had also not done much with the little she was given.

"I will repent, and I will try to be more charitable to your father. You must understand he developed quite a reputation."

He nodded, walking around to sit at his desk. A mahogany piece, carved with fleur-de-lis all the way from France. "I know that very well.

"I am not him, and yet people expect me to be. I am content living in the country. Trust me when I say that, but I cannot. People have expectations of me. My father requires me to continue the family work. These last few months have been a respite for me. I have done many things I would rather not have done."

She walked over to him, placing a hand on each of his shoulders. Feeling how tense he was, she pressed her thumbs on the area and began kneading.

A tiny groan escaped his lips and she kissed his head.

"I am sorry to have added to your stress. You do not need to hear such talk from me. I promised you I would be bonny in the trough and bed. I have failed in both."

His hand patted hers.

"Only because you have gotten yourself with child so quickly," he said teasingly. "In many respects you are the perfect wife. Too bad I miss your company in the evenings."

"At least you may go visit the brothels," she said lightly.

He scoffed. "I have not in a long time. Fear of the pox is too great. I don't think it is worth the risk for one moment's pleasure."

"More men should think like you. But I would not

mind. I understand that it cannot be easy for you." Even as she said it she knew it was not true. But she was being realistic. What man stayed faithful to his wife? Her previous had been known to pester the maids, especially when she had been with child.

Like all women before her and that would come after, she had tried to turn a blind eye. If she had truly loved him like Queen Katherine of Aragon had, perhaps she would have been heartbroken and made a fuss over it. But, besides a sense of disgust, she had been very little affected.

From a young age she had learned that men strayed. Her mother had been a reputed beauty, but her father had been little better than a lecher. When he was caught in Edward's wife's bed she had not been surprised that he would betray his wife. She had been horrified about who he had chosen to do it with. It seemed men did not respect the sanctity of marriage like women did.

Often it was a refuge for women. In a life when a woman had but three choices, it was often the most appealing, and the king was taking away the choice to join a nunnery.

They reached Hampton Court. Parliament was in session and the king would make his appearance. They were trying to settle the matter of the succession and religion.

King Henry VIII wanted to cement the religious changes he'd implemented into law.

Her sister had dark circles under her eyes. That was

the first thing she noticed when she was announced at her doors.

Against her pale skin they seemed to look more like bruises.

She did her the courtesy of pretending to not have noticed.

The ladies of the bedchamber greeted her with half-smiles, all their eyes traveling quickly from her face to her growing belly. She heard many whispers of "how easily the peasants breed" as she approached her sister.

She had worn a black gown today, as it concealed her bulging stomach somewhat. She did not want to draw attention to herself, but she had succeeded in doing the opposite. The other ladies were in creams and light pallid colours, so she stood out.

Anne Herbert vacated the seat next to her sister and she sat down.

"You are looking well," she said, lying smoothly. "How big you have grown. Does he keep you up at night?"

Jane nodded, a hand to her belly. "He seems most awake just as soon as my head hits the pillow, and when I can fall asleep I am soon awoken by the need to use the chamber pot."

Elizabeth gave her a sympathetic look.

"It is a good sign though. My own little Henry was the same when I was with child. Soon all your struggles will be over."

Jane rubbed a hand over her belly. Her hand was

nearly as pale as the white lace embroidered with gold threads of her sleeves.

Elizabeth worried for her even more but tried not to say anything or look too long at her.

"Have you been outside much? Perhaps a walk in the gardens would cheer you."

Jane shook her head. "The king and I are fearful of the plague. It hit the city hard this summer, and I would not wish to endanger my life over a walk."

Ah, so that was why she seemed paler than usual.

"Well, a bit of fresh air now couldn't hurt. We could sit by the window." She stood, as though she wanted to help her sister up.

Jane shook her head again.

"The draft would be bad for my health."

Elizabeth couldn't help looking exasperated but knew she was fighting a losing battle and she didn't say another word.

They sat embroidering the hems of baby gowns all morning.

Occasionally, she would force Jane to pause and to eat bits and pieces every now and then.

Her sister would grow mad with worry if she had become so fearful of every little thing. Could she not see how pale and wan she looked? Did no one dare tell her?

She voiced these concerns to Edward, who was in too good of a mood to concern himself too much. He was quite pleased with the direction he assumed he had taken the family.

Elizabeth didn't like the way the power and influence had all gone to his head.

He was practically cocky.

"Edward, you must see how ill she looks. That would be contrary to what all our efforts have been up to this point," she said, pressing him. "Anne did not look so sickly with her first child."

"Anne is younger. Our sister is just quiet and pale. She always was. You always teased her about it," he pointed out a bit rudely.

Elizabeth felt the familiar twinge of guilt when it came to her sister. She had been unfair to her. That much she could admit.

"Please, you must encourage her to go outside before her confinement. I think it is bad for her to be cooped up so much. Her worries are so unfounded. They will drive her mad."

"I will ask the doctors to speak to her," Edward said at last. "Since you are so concerned. But she is in the care of the best ladies of the land and has many midwives. The king is taking no chances."

Elizabeth bit back the response: as opposed to all the other times? But she had won a minor victory.

"Who will go into confinement with her? Perhaps Mary Shelton should go too."

Watching her brother's face twist into a grimace made Elizabeth realize what was displeasing him so much.

"Even if she does, it does not mean that she could not leave the rooms. So if you are doing it as a way to prevent the king from going to her, then you are sorely mistaken. Let him have his fun with her. She is not a risk to us."

"It's how it always was. I worry about someone else catching his eye, especially if he is disappointed." Despite him keeping his voice low, Elizabeth's hand instinctively whipped out and gripped his wrist to silence him, applying pleasure.

"She is carrying a healthy son. I have felt him move. It could not be denied," she said, stressing every word.

"Of course. I am sorry I spoke. It has been a very stressful last few weeks and Thomas has been of no help, more like a thorn in my side. Only our dear brother Henry is helpful to me."

Elizabeth crossed her arms in front of her.

"And what am I? Furniture? I thought I was quite helpful."

He laughed. "No, no you are. I spoke out of turn. But Henry looks after our family estates, and even you are hard at work in the queen's rooms. You've done well with your marriage—that any fool could see. But Thomas? He just gambles and swaggers around court batting his eyes at anything with two legs. I worry about him. He asks for something to do, but I cannot trust him with it. I fear he tries to undermine me."

"What happened to our family unity? We cannot have competition and fighting amongst ourselves."

Edward shrugged, looking at the ceiling.

"I suppose we are no different from any other human. We are sinful creatures, though we try to be good."

Elizabeth sighed too. Exasperated by this news more

than anything. It was hard enough worrying about Jane and her own pregnancy, and now to have to worry about her brothers too?

"I cannot wait to go back to the country."

"Really?"

She gave him a look. "Of course. I am back for two days and it seems like the roof is about to cave in here. How can I tolerate this?" She placed a hand to her own belly. "I have to think of myself and my child too."

He seemed to consider her. "Well, you may have your wish. I hope you shall be happy, but I, and I am sure Jane as well, appreciate you coming. A friendly face makes all the difference. The court can be a spiteful pit of vipers."

"Don't I know it. I cannot seem to enter a room without comments."

"It comes with marrying a Cromwell. Willingly," he teased.

Rearranging the skirts of her gown, she smiled. "Well, I shall have to learn to endure it, then.

"Other than that you are well?" she asked him.

He nodded. "I am growing anxious about the outcome with our sister, but of course there is nothing we can do now but pray for her. Anne is in good spirits. She saw baby Henry settled into his nursery. I hear my little niece and nephew have joined you. Are you sure that is wise?"

"I enjoy having them near at hand. I will send them back to Oakham Hall if there is any disquiet in the city. But I couldn't bear to be parted from them yet again."

He nodded, but Elizabeth knew he didn't truly understand.

"Speaking of which, I should go see them now. My Henry will be needing a tutor soon. Speaking of which, I think there are too many Henrys in our family now. Gregory says if this child is a boy then we shall name him Henry as well to honour the king." She smiled at the ridiculousness of it. "Can you imagine the confusion?"

Edward laughed. "I can indeed."

Days progressed slowly. During the day she tended to her sister and then she would take the barge downriver to spend some time with her children before they went to bed.

Her father-in-law was keeping her husband busy and she rarely saw him. Perhaps he was displeased with her in some way.

Maybe he didn't like that she had brought her children to court.

There were plenty of reasons for him to be upset, but she did not think much about it. As Gregory said, he was their friend not their foe. She had to erase all her prejudices about him.

The weather was beginning to become chilly and, unfortunately, she caught a cold on her way to and fro between court and Austin Friars.

Elizabeth was forbidden from visiting the court until

she was well again. Gregory came to keep her company, fearing for their child.

"As you can see, I am quite well. It is just a runny nose and a slight cough."

"You don't have a fever?" he said, pressing a hand to her forehead.

She knew he was worried about the sweating sickness that seemed to spread throughout the city, but no, it could not be.

"I am well, and your child is well too," she said, taking his hand and pressing it to her belly, where their child moved and kicked ferociously.

He was surprised, nearly jumping back.

"Does that not hurt?"

She shook her head. "No, although it can make it hard to fall asleep. He's an active little one."

"You think it will be a boy?"

"Maybe, just a feeling I have. This pregnancy is much like when I carried Henry. I did not have morning sickness with Margery, so perhaps it is a boy. Would you care?"

Gregory shrugged. "I just hope the both of you will be well. My mother had me and two daughters. Even if it is not a boy now, it could be one later. And if we only have daughters, then I will see them married off to someone worthy. And if we have no children, then I shall adopt one of my cousins."

Her laughter filled the room. "If only more men were as generous as you."

"I don't have much to lose, I guess. There are no

ancestors that are looking down from heaven right now displeased with me. Already my father has accomplished more than all of our forebearers had added up together."

"And you shall do more still. I have no doubt."

His smile was strained. "I fear I don't have it in me, but I won't be given much of a choice. My father would as soon wring my neck."

She tilted her head. "I thought I was to think well of him now. That hardly makes it sound promising."

He grinned. "I spoke out of turn then. But you must understand: as my father's only son, there's a lot of pressure put upon me. People expect me to know things like he does. But I do not have the heart to delve deep into people's minds to discover their secrets. My father is a natural statesman. He has spoiled me in my youth, and now I am as soft and good-tempered as those gentlemen he despises."

"Ah, so it is his fault, then." Elizabeth grinned like a Cheshire cat. "Watch out, husband. This little child will soon be blaming you for all his problems too."

He waved her off. "I have been forewarned. Now I shall go tell the cook to make you a nice thick broth and make sure your maid sits with you while you drink it all."

"Where do you think you are going to?" She pouted.

"Work to attend to, of course, and I will be wanted back at court."

"Not if I cough on you. I doubt they will let you back until I am well again. Don't you know how paranoid they've become?"

He frowned. "It sounds like you are making excuses."

Elizabeth's sly smile was wiped away. "Well, I may have been joking, but I am serious, husband. I urge you to send a messenger. Your business can be done from here just as well as it can be done from court."

"Careful, Lady Elizabeth, some might think you are so desperate for my company because you have fallen in love with me."

"They shall never know." She pushed him off her bed with a hearty shove. "Take care of me because I am ailing and the doctors have ordered me not to leave this bed."

She caught the way he rolled his eyes as he stood and walked out of the room, but she smiled to herself, amused that she and her husband were so compatible with each other. What a happy accident.

Finally recovered, Elizabeth helped to oversee the preparation of the lying-in chambers. She had elbowed her way into the position, but for once Jane assented that she should be left in charge. Perhaps Jane was not in the mood for a fight.

Elizabeth oversaw everything from the linen brought in to the way they cleaned out the rushes in the room and replaced them. Pictures of saints and relics were brought in, and a heap of firewood and candles stored away in the cupboards for when they would be needed.

The windows too were boarded up. Only one would be able to be opened to allow light and fresh air in. But

Elizabeth doubted Jane would permit them even that much.

Lastly, the crib enamelled with pure gold was carried in. The king had designed it himself. It was a shockingly expensive thing, but nothing was too good for the future king of England.

Elizabeth could only frown. Such things simply reminded Jane of all the expectations laid at her feet. She did not look strong enough to be able to meet them. She barely had the energy to feed herself.

At her farewell feast the king did not seem to notice this. He kept petting and pawing at her as though she was his favoured hound, but his eyes were roving over the eligible young ladies dancing before them.

If Jane cared, she did not show any sign.

Elizabeth wished for an ounce of her patience.

Gregory came to pull her aside.

"My father wishes to speak to you."

"Why?" She was frowning. "I haven't done anything, I swear."

He looked amused for a moment, but his expression was serious. "Come along, sweetheart."

She allowed him to lead her away down the long galleries to the minister's offices. He should have been at the feast, except he wasn't. He was at his desk, a pen in hand.

"Lady Elizabeth, have a seat. I hope you are doing well," he said without looking up.

Elizabeth looked from the chair to her husband. Was

this an interrogation? He gave her a nudge and she took her seat.

"I see you are growing plump and cheerful in your most happy condition," Thomas Cromwell said, giving her a scrutinizing glance and then looking to her husband. "I chose well for you. The two of you seem well suited."

"What do you mean, sir?" she said.

He was looking back down at the letters in front of him. "Oh, it was Gregory here who suggested you might welcome a match with him. But I had already been talking to your brother about it for quite some time. I assumed that you would be easier to manage if the two of you had time to lock eyes in the corridors and form an attachment. It is always good to have informants in every house in England, so I thought the marriage was a very good idea. You had not wanted to work with me, but I found a way around it in such a way that would work well for everyone. So tell me I had not been wrong to think this was a good alliance to make." He fixed her with one of those gazes that made her forget her own words. It cut her to her core, and she was fighting with herself to keep from trembling. She felt used. But this wasn't the time to start crying. She exhaled.

"I don't understand what you are alluding to," she said at last.

"Shall I put it more bluntly? Is your sister well?"

Before she could speak, a hand shot up.

"No, don't tell me a lie. Tell me the truth. In my

rooms you can speak openly," he said with a soothing undertone.

She stopped herself from biting her lip but a moment too late. Cromwell had caught the movement, despite appearing distracted by his papers. He nodded.

"It is plain to see she does not look well. The king is planning to ride to Greenwich."

"But the chambers are prepared here at Hampton Court. I am confused."

"Are you indeed? Think about what I have just said for a moment longer and it will all make sense."

There was a long ominous pause, and into that pause all her anxieties and worries surfaced.

"The king is leaving her? He is abandoning her?"

"In a way, yes." Cromwell tilted his head. He looked like he was about to reach across the table and take her hands in his.

She pulled them off the table, hiding them in the folds of her gown.

"She has done nothing wrong," Elizabeth said softly, grief heavy in her voice.

"No. No one is accusing her of having done anything wrong. Although you have been unable to keep her from irritating the king on occasion. Her comments are not forgotten. The king does not appreciate being gainsaid by his wife, especially in public." He looked as though he might sigh, but he was too much a master of himself to do so.

"My sister was doing what she thought was right. It is a queen's duty to be merciful. I thought all that was forgotten." Elizabeth pressed forward as though haggling at a market.

"It does not matter. What matters is what he thinks. In any case, he is waiting anxiously for the birth of his child, but as you can see, he is anxious and it seems as though Jane has given him cause to be anxious."

"She could not have done," Elizabeth interjected, not caring how rude it was.

"Have you looked at your sister recently?" Cromwell looked tired, as tired as perhaps Jane did.

"Yes, she is tired. They have filled her head with horror stories. She cannot help but be worried over every little thing. She almost yelled when she thought she had eaten a prune. Some woman had told her they cause babies to be born with skins as wrinkly as their skin," Elizabeth said, trying to explain. "She is caught up in everything. She was always pale, but of course being told that a morning chill might kill the baby inside her has made her stay indoors."

"Does she not see how well you fare? Why would she not take your advice?" Cromwell pressed.

Elizabeth leaned back. "I am her younger sister," she said, as though that explained everything.

His nod was slow, his expression exasperated with the troubles of women that he had no control over.

Elizabeth looked to Gregory, who was leaning against the back of her chair, a thoughtful look on his face, but he did not rush to her defence or speak up for Jane. What did she expect? After all, wasn't he the one who had been manipulating her all this time? Using her for information, even if it was at his father's command.

"There is nothing actually wrong with her except that someone has knowingly or unknowingly fed her fears and she has made herself unwell," Elizabeth said with a tone of finality. "You will see. She will give birth to a son and win back the king's favour."

"He has heard that being promised before," Cromwell pointed out.

"But never from a true wife," Elizabeth shot back.

The grim expression broke into a grin at her bravery.

"Very well, Lady Elizabeth. Forgive me for troubling you. Try to do your best for your sister, but know that she is on precarious ground and do teach her to curb her tongue. Her husband is not as understanding as yours."

She stood, smoothing out her gown in order to wipe the sweat off her hands. She didn't know why this rather portly man before her could incite such fears. But she had seen how he could make or break a family. She feared that the power he yielded could be turned against them.

"Oh, and I heard little Henry was asking for a horse. I have a pony ready for him whenever you would think it is time for him to start learning to ride," he added as a parting shot.

Her hand froze on the door handle. It was irritating and frightening how he seemed to know so much about the most mundane of matters. She looked at Gregory. His face was a blank slate. Was he really telling his father everything? It would make sense, but...

She bowed her head forward. "I thank you. Henry will be pleased to know."

Cromwell gave her a toothy smile, all politeness.

"Next time, I trust you to answer me with the truth right away. No need to dance around it." He had picked up the quill and began scratching away at a fresh sheet of paper.

Elizabeth left the room as quickly as she was able to, thanking her lucky stars she wasn't any bigger than she was now. Her heart was racing. She was infuriated.

There was no way she could carry this news to her family. They would likely find out eventually, but she didn't want to be the bearer of bad news. The messenger always seemed to get shot in situations like these. More than that, her sister needed to try to scrounge up some optimism for the work ahead. It was never easy facing childbed. Many never rose from it.

֍

She refused to see Gregory until she had calmed down. She had treated him coldly, as though he was a piece of dust that refused to be cleaned. She blamed him for conspiring with his father. For not standing up to him. For bringing her into that room. Her anger had turned into fury that roiled in her stomach and caused her poor child to kick and squirm in her belly.

For this child she would have to be calm. She tried her best because her sister needed her now.

She was playing with Margery, a game of catch with

a tiny wooden ball that she had liked to chew on as a child, when a tap at the nursery door broke their game.

The door opened and Gregory stepped in, looking peevish.

Elizabeth looked away from him immediately, not wishing to see his face. He must have known that she would not start screaming and arguing with him in front of her children.

But that did not mean she had to pay any attention to him.

She continued playing the little game as Gregory watched from the corner of the room until Margery walked over to him, handing the ball to him to see. The little traitor, Elizabeth thought as she stood up from her seat.

"It's a very nice ball. Do you know what colour it is?" Gregory said, trying to speak to her.

Margery babbled something incoherent.

"She doesn't speak much yet. She wouldn't know her colours," Elizabeth informed him.

"We will have to teach her, then," he said, ruffling the girl's dark mop of hair.

Elizabeth frowned at the gesture, but Margery giggled and reached for the ball he held out for her.

"Will you go on ignoring me for the rest of the day?"

"The rest of my life if I so choose," she said.

"I am sure you would. Try not to take it to heart. It is better you knew and weren't surprised by the news. Now you can better prepare your sister."

"You think I would go to her with this news? Even if

it wasn't so grave I would dare not. My sister is living in terror of failure. How could I tell her that the odds are against her? I thought you were smarter than this," she said as calmly as she could, but she couldn't keep all the anger and malice from her tone.

Margery looked at her, a pout forming on her face.

"Mama?"

Elizabeth forced herself to smile and bent down to be at eye level with her.

"Don't worry, darling. It's nothing. Shall we play some more?"

Margery nodded.

Elizabeth turned her back on Gregory, not wishing to continue the conversation.

She could not disappear for the whole day. They would be progressing to the darkened chambers prepared for her sister, and she would step inside that dark place with her.

"When do you think you will forgive me?"

Elizabeth shrugged. "Is there anything to forgive? I am simply angry at myself for believing for a moment that this marriage was more than just a political tool. I wish I never came to care for you or fall for your charms. They are false."

"I do not deny that my father encouraged me to form an attachment to you. But I truly do care about you. I have not the strength to stand up to him, but I do what I can," he said, a hand waving over her children as though to imply he had tried to get her everything she could have wanted.

It was true that he had, but now the gesture felt sullied. As if he had been planning to apologize to her for quite some time.

"Then we can call ourselves even and have nothing to do with each other from here on out," she snapped.

Elizabeth saw immediately how her words stung him and she wanted to reach out to him. To say that she forgave him now, but she couldn't. She didn't truly, and she wasn't about to make him feel better at her expense. She'd had enough of doing that with her brothers growing up.

She settled on sending him a note when she got the chance. She needed her space. Now she needed to return to the court and take her place in the train of ladies escorting the queen to her rooms.

Elizabeth watched as Henry kissed Jane before the whole assembly when they reached the door of her darkened chambers.

A few private words passed between them.

Jane performed a little curtsy and was taken inside.

It would have been sweet to see had Elizabeth not known that the very next day Henry was to ride out to enjoy the hunting at Greenwich. He wanted to have nothing to do with this business if it went poorly.

Elizabeth followed her sister, who had already sat down by the fireside, a prayer book in hand.

So it was Elizabeth who took to walking around the room, looking over all the little details and making sure all was at hand.

She had gone into confinement twice. It was dull.

There was nothing to do really, and the room was too dark to try to do much needlework. Unless one wanted to strain her eyesight. She hoped Jane would not try.

"Well, this is lovely," Anne Herbert commented. Elizabeth saw her examining the crib of gold plate.

"Everything in honour of the new baby to be born," someone else commented. As though explaining to her.

They settled in. Six ladies would be sleeping directly in these rooms with the midwives in an adjoining room. Until the birth, they would be dining well and drinking the finest England had to offer. It was a coveted post.

Elizabeth would be sent out on little errands to send messages. Oftentimes she snuck out to see her children and was gone for longer, but she needed to see them too. Being stuck in those dark rooms was not good for her health.

On the day her sister discovered that the king had left the palace, Elizabeth wrote to Gregory to ask him to meet her when possible.

They walked along the gallery, admiring the portraits hanging in the halls.

He was waiting for her to speak and finally, after taking a deep breath, she did.

"I am not as mad as I was a few days ago, but you must understand why I was so upset. Tell me this wasn't any of your doing."

He shook his head. "It wasn't. My father should have handled you more gently. He likes you. Told me so himself."

"I felt hounded for information."

Gregory sighed. "My father is under a lot of stress. A lot is riding on this, and to see the state of the queen you would hardly think it is likely that this would be a good outcome. As I am sure it will be, but it is not unfair to be concerned."

She let out a breath of air to steady herself.

"It feels unfair. It makes me angry. It is not as though Jane chose this."

Gregory nodded. "I know that, but the point is to placate the king."

"And what of my sister? Who is placating her? Who is her champion?"

"You are, my dear, and a very good one at that."

"What is my brother Edward doing?" she asked, ignoring his attempt at both a joke and a compliment.

"He is pretending all is well."

Elizabeth was exasperated. They stopped in front of a portrait of Margaret Beaufort. Here was a lady who was proof that miracles could happen. She had been married so young that when she gave birth they did not think she would live. She defied all expectations and years later, with barely any support, she had managed to put her son on the throne.

Elizabeth should try to be more optimistic.

"I am sorry we have quarrelled. But I cannot pretend that I am not angry with you. If you want I can try to smile and be merry, but it is not what I feel in my heart."

He nodded. "I understand. How is our child?"

"Growing well. Restless, as I am in that dark confinement chamber, but at least I am still allowed to leave."

"If it is too much for you, let me know."

Elizabeth gave him a look that said what could he do? It was clearer than ever that he was his father's pawn.

He escorted her back to the doors of the queen's chambers. His hand lingered over hers and she could tell he wanted to kiss her, but she pulled away, walking through the doors before he had the chance.

Elizabeth had come to realize that as smart and clever as he was, Gregory was his father's son. His loyalty was to him. She wasn't sure why she had come to expect something different.

When did a tumble in the sheets ever buy proper loyalty?

⁂

Weeks passed and her sister showed no signs of going into labour. Her baby still moved well, so there was no worry about something being wrong with the baby. Perhaps she had been mistaken about the dates.

The king sent messages through one of the gentlemen of his chamber. He never came himself, however, and this seemed to pain Jane.

In the evenings, when Jane found she could not sleep, Elizabeth sat by her side, plaiting her hair in long thick braids.

"You must prove everyone wrong."

"Pardon?" Her voice sounded very far away.

"The king loves you. You shall show him that you can give him a strong healthy child."

Jane put a hand to her belly. The child gave a big kick and she winced. "That is not hard to imagine. I wish that he would be more optimistic. It feels like everyone talks about me as though I am not here."

"They are worrying about how to take care of you better. They are worried because of all that has come before. But you cannot worry. As we all know, those were not marriages blessed by God."

"Queen Katherine was a godly woman," Jane remarked.

"Yes, she was, but she was not truly married to the king," Elizabeth said, pressing the point home. It was not something she personally believed, but she needed her sister to believe it.

"Yes," came the weak reply.

"Good, so there's no reason why anything should go wrong with you."

Jane seemed to be avoiding looking at her. Elizabeth buckled down.

"Jane, all will be well with you. You must believe that."

A smile broke across Jane's sour expression. "If you command it, then I must obey."

Elizabeth hesitated and, realizing she had been grasping Jane's hands, released them.

"It has always been like this since we were young. You were almost eight years my junior, yet you always seemed to know more than me. Often you proved to be correct. So I shall listen to you," Jane said, trying her best to be reassuring.

"I am sorry."

"For what?" Jane tilted her head as though truly confused and uncertain.

"I have not always been the kindest of sisters. I have been resentful. I see how you suffer…"

"I am not your confessor, Elizabeth. No one is perfect and I do not suffer. I am reported to be the happiest woman in all of Christendom. Or perhaps you have not heard."

The dry humour in her sister's voice made her laugh. She was surprised to find her eyes wet with tears.

"Do not cry. Your husband will be very upset with me if you do." Jane wiped them away.

Elizabeth wanted very much at this moment to embrace her sister and let her stroke her head as she used to do when she was nursing her through the illnesses of childhood.

Jane was always too kind to a fault.

But custom prevented her, even among such close relations. Jane was still queen, even though she was uncrowned.

"I have a letter from Lady Mary. She wishes to join me in my confinement chamber, and I wrote to her giving my permission," Jane said, as though she had just remembered.

"The two of you have grown very close," Elizabeth said, now that she had gotten a hold of herself. "I am sure her mother would have liked to know that her daughter is well looked after by you."

"Yes, and she is a suitable companion to me. The king

says I should learn to be more queenly. He scolds me that I have the manners of a country lady."

Elizabeth frowned. "That's what he used to say was so charming about you. I am sure you are mistaken."

Jane merely shrugged. "I can never please him lately. Perhaps in this I can." A hand went to her belly, the fingertips lightly grazing the swell. Almost as though she thought her belly was too fragile to touch. The child in there was so precious.

"This baby is yours as much as his," Elizabeth said with a frown.

"It is England's. I am merely the vessel."

"You are his mother, and your love has given him life thus far. A child never truly forgets their mother, and I daresay you shall be a doting one." Elizabeth couldn't help contradicting her.

Jane wasn't listening. She was picking at some threads sticking out at the seams of her gown.

Elizabeth had tried. She hoped she had gotten through to her. Somewhat. She would never wish to be queen. Not now that she saw what it was doing to her sister.

CHAPTER SEVEN

Her sister's labour pains began during the night just as she had finished praying at her prie-dieu.

As she stood she had let out a loud startled cry as the first of many contractions hit her. Luckily, many pairs of hands were available and she did not topple forward.

The ladies all looked at each other. Surely, this was a good sign. God was smiling upon Jane.

The midwives were called in. Hot pots of water were boiling. A special spiced wine was being thrown together. The operation moved like clockwork. To an outsider it might have seemed like a disorderly mess, but everyone had their place and knew their task.

Lady Mary clutched Jane's left hand while Elizabeth stubbornly took her right hand.

News was sent to the king.

First they began walking her, but that quickly exhausted Jane and she was laid back on the bed as her pains came faster and faster, but there was no baby. Her water had not even broken yet.

By morning her sister had not advanced any further in her labour, though she pushed and hauled on the rope as best she could.

They tried to feed her broth and the spiced wine.

As evening approached, the midwives began to try to use all the tricks they had in their arsenal. They threw pepper in her face to make her sneeze. They rubbed her back. They forced her to walk. Nothing.

On the second day, Elizabeth was ready to faint as well. She had not slept, refusing to leave her sister's side. It was clear Jane had not been able to rest either. Her pains came too frequently for that to happen.

The doctors arrived.

They conferred with the midwives. They looked anxiously at the queen and made their suggestions through the screen. They did not actually look upon the sacred person of the queen.

They passed over potions and powders for Jane to take. She took them dutifully, although half were thrown up mere moments later.

"Where is the king?" Jane asked her once.

Elizabeth did not have the heart to tell her he had not come. Her sister's tear-stained face was nearly unrecognizable, twisted with pain for so long.

"He is waiting to see you both. You must be strong. You can do this," Elizabeth whispered into her ears.

The words seemed to comfort her.

The midwives at the foot of the bed were arguing if

they should pile up the fire to increase the heat in the room or open the window to let the crisp autumn air in.

Fools, Elizabeth thought to herself.

Their next visitor was the Archbishop Cranmer. An ill sign.

She wanted to prevent him coming to her sister's bedside.

"Lady Elizabeth, step aside. I do this out of kindness."

Fresh tears from anger and exhaustion were streaming down her face.

"You will be the death of her. She will know what your coming means."

"I am here to bring spiritual comfort and to give her the last rites. It might help strengthen her, and if not then she would be able to ascend to heaven. God forbid," he said in an undertone.

Elizabeth shook her head. Her vision becoming blurry.

"No."

"Lady, you are unwell."

Elizabeth wasn't sure what happened next. She remembered feeling like she was swimming in a hazy fog. All she wanted was to see this intruder out of here.

"She's waking up."

Elizabeth blinked once, twice. She remembered where she was. Her head was still swimming, but she focused on Lady Anne's face. She was holding a cup to her lips.

"What happened?" she asked, finding her voice at last.

"I don't know. You were talking to the archbishop and then you fainted. I was told to watch you. You should not be here in your condition."

"She is my sister," Elizabeth said, frowning. Then she heard the cries and tried to stand. "I should go to her."

"Finish this. I advise you rest. Your sister is almost at the end of her troubles. The baby is coming."

"At long last, God preserve us."

"Amen."

Elizabeth, invigorated by the news, drank as much of the drink as she could muster and then rushed to her sister's side.

Many people were crowded around her, urging her onward. Jane's eyes were half-closed, but her expression was set in stern determination.

"I see the head, Your Grace," a midwife called out. The crowd of women shifted and Elizabeth could see the blood.

Her stomach roiled. There was so much blood.

Never mind, she thought to herself and walked over to her sister's side, not caring who she had to push out of the way.

She took hold of one of her hands, letting her sister squeeze her arms. The grip was so tight she felt her bones creaking, but she did not complain. A midwife nodded to her.

"Time to push again, Your Grace," she said.

Jane mumbled something incoherent. Elizabeth's gaze snapped to her face. She seemed barely lucid.

"Jane, you are doing so well. Now push. Push, Your Majesty," she said, her voice urgent and forceful.

Jane seemed to heed her and gave a final push.

"That's it. One more time!"

"Jane, once more. Try with all your might. You can do this. This is your destiny." Elizabeth wasn't even sure she knew what she was saying.

One final push and suddenly there was a new cry joining her sister's.

"You've done it, Your Grace."

Jane fell back on the pillows, her mouth hanging open and panting in her exhaustion. Elizabeth was handed a cool cloth, and she dabbed at her sister's face.

The cord was snipped.

"What is it?" Jane asked. She too could hear the cries. "My child, is he well?"

All the ladies in the room were looking at each other in amazement and wonderment, letting the midwife bring the babe, still bloodied but wrapped in a white cloth.

"Your son, Your Grace. Well done." The midwife presented him to her.

Fresh tears sprang to Jane's eyes and she reached out a wavering hand to her son.

"We must clean him, Your Grace."

She put her hand down, nodding. "I am so tired, Elizabeth."

"You've done well," Elizabeth said, unaware that she was crying herself. Jane had done it, against all odds.

"Send a message to his majesty. He would want to know," Elizabeth said, not caring who had the honour.

There was a scramble to be the first out of the room with the news.

The midwives were scrambling to clean both mother and baby.

One pulled her to the side.

"There is a lot of bleeding, milady. You should ask the physicians to make her a draft. She was in labour for so long."

Elizabeth bit her lip, nodding. She knew first-hand how dangerous this was. The bed linen her sister was resting on was drenched irreparably in her blood. She was nervous for her, but she knew from her own birth that this was normal. To some extent.

They worked for the rest of the night to stop the bleeding. At one point Jane lost consciousness, but that was hardly surprising given how she had not slept in over two days.

When she came to, she was given porridge thickened with bone broth. She ate and seemed to recover a bit. Throughout it all a smile was plastered on her face.

She had done her duty.

Elizabeth was pulled away at last by Anne Herbert.

"The king is on his way, traveling hard on the road. Your husband bids you come out of the room now to rest. You have your own child to look after. I am to pull you kicking and screaming if I have to," she said to her.

Elizabeth did not want to fight her.

She said her farewells to Jane, who was slipping off to sleep again.

The mattress had been replaced and fresh bed linen laid out. Fresh herbs burned in the fire to hide the scent of blood in the room.

In the main hall, Gregory was waiting with her maid, carrying a tray heaped with food.

"Fresh from the kitchen," he said when he caught her looking at it. "Now, I am going to take you to rest and make sure you eat everything. I should never have let you come in your condition."

He shook his head. "And don't think I did not hear from the archbishop of your little spat that resulted in you fainting."

Elizabeth blinked, a bit confused. "Did we? I don't quite remember." She was a bit embarrassed. "I am so tired. What was he doing there…" Then it came back to her. Piece by piece. "Never mind. I remember and I don't regret anything."

"Yes, I can see that. Nor do I expect you to make amends," Gregory said. She hated when he was like this, as though he knew her mind.

"Well, let's get you off your feet," he said, holding out his arm to her.

So while her sister was receiving the congratulations of her husband and the cannons on the Tower of London were shut off, Elizabeth ate her fill and let her exhaustion hit her. She was lulled off into sleep.

When she awoke at noon the next day, Gregory was there with another tray of food.

"You've become my errand boy," she said, rubbing the sleep from her eyes.

"This time I wasn't the one who fetched it, but once you eat, if you are feeling better, you should try to get dressed so you won't miss all the festivities," he said. Then, setting down the tray beside her, he took a seat by her bedside, apparently keeping her company as she ate. She could look at him more kindly.

"Is everyone happy?" she asked, looking at the plate of food and nibbling on some fresh bread. A meat pie was particularly appetizing to her right now as well.

"Oh yes, the presents have begun flowing in. Your brother is to be made an earl, or at least that's the rumour my father heard."

"An earl?" Elizabeth was amazed indeed.

"My father is overjoyed. Your family all are too. Jane is likely to be crowned as soon as she is churched." He began listing off the lists. "A great christening is under way. Of course everything was planned out beforehand, but..."

"Nothing was prepared to save on the expense in case it all went wrong?" she finished for him before biting into the soft crust.

"Something like that. But you are well?"

She nodded.

"I need to get clean and into fresh clothes. I feel like I have a year's worth of grime and muck on me. They heated up that room so much I'm surprised we didn't all roast alive."

Gregory laughed. "I am glad your sense of humour is

back. The children want to see you too. You disappeared for four days, and it seems they have gotten used to seeing you."

"Of course, once I am properly dressed." She got off the bed but had stood too fast and was dizzy with fatigue, nearly falling over herself.

Gregory caught her and suddenly they were very close to one another, closer than they had been in weeks. She could feel her cheeks colouring as she thought of his strong arms wrapped around her.

Her lips parted, about to say something, when Gregory's lips came crashing down on hers. It was a hurried kiss, as though he feared she would pull away at any second, but when she didn't it became more gentle and pliant.

"I am sorry, can we not make amends?" he said.

"I suppose we shall. Whether I want it or not, we are tied together," she said, a bit unkindly.

"I truly have come to care for you. I do not want you to think ill of me."

"And I don't. But I know where your loyalty lies. Hopefully, you will afford our child more once it is born. Don't worry, it is not a criticism. I know the way of the world. The fact that you are here by my side and not at the king's raking in favours as the uncle to the new prince of Wales means a great deal to me."

He seemed to understand. He did not contradict her because that would have been a lie, and at the very least he was not that. She appreciated him even more.

"You are a good man, Gregory," she said. "If only we

were both born poor farmers, then we could have had a different sort of life not chasing after intrigues and plotting. We would have been content to work in the fields in the summer, and then to starve by the fire in the winter."

"I'm sure some kind lord would send out alms for us to see us through."

Her smile was cool.

He kissed her forehead again. "I accept your terms. I hope you will still find my company enjoyable in the future. Now get dressed, for our work is not done yet."

Deciding that dressing in her now favoured dark gown would not be suitable, considering the joyous triumph of her sister, she picked out a bright blue damask gown. A new one made for her before she had discovered she was with child. Her maid helped her slip it on, loosening the girdle as much as possible.

Her hair was brushed and pulled up with a net before the gable hood was pinned in place. This was a new one, from her husband. Pearls and diamonds sparkled on it. She looked every bit like the sister of a queen and no longer like a pauper at court.

Her children were excited by her reappearance and would not let her go, even though she had only intended to visit them a short while. In the end, she had to bribe them with promises of cake.

On her way to her sister's rooms the corridors were packed with people. A yeoman of the guard had to lead the way to allow her to go through. As a lady of the bedchamber, she was given the privilege.

She looked behind her as the doors closed behind her. Had the court doubled in size?

There was great cheer in the room as she came in. The air felt bright, and everyone walking by had an air of success about them.

"Has everyone given birth to the king's son?" she asked Anne, her brother's wife, who appeared at her side to greet her with an embrace.

Her twinkling laughter told Elizabeth that she had probably had a cup or two of wine.

"What a thing to say, Lady Elizabeth. But we are celebrating. It is to be a holiday. All we could ever hope for is at our feet."

"How is my sister? And the baby?"

"He is well. They are to name him Edward. He was born on St. Edward's day. Had you realized?"

Elizabeth shook her head. She wasn't very clear what today's date was at the moment.

"He's blond, like Jane, but you can see the king's features in his face. His majesty has ordered nothing but the best for his little son. He certainly spared no expense," she said to her.

Elizabeth did not tell her that she could tell her the exact sum. She had seen the papers. Gregory had done most of the calculations while his father worked on some other tasks. It was Gregory who had ordered everything that would be needed for a prince of Wales.

There were guards at every door, a small army of nursemaids, and the best wet nurses. His gold cradle was only the beginning of the wealth he was given. He would have a very privileged life, and hopefully he would thrive and one day in the distant future take the throne as King Edward VI.

"I cannot wait to see him," Elizabeth said after a moment. "I wish I had not taken ill myself."

Anne patted her hand. "Well, you overburdened yourself, but it was all worth the effort. Come, I can take you to him."

Elizabeth let her lead the way away from Jane's chambers and through double doors to the adjoining nursery.

"The king wants to send his son to begin living at Richmond as soon as he is christened. He's already set up his household."

Knowing this was the protocol, Elizabeth did not comment, but she herself would hate it.

"I am sure my sister will miss him," Elizabeth couldn't help but comment.

"Well, she shall have another soon. We all hope. The king is so pleased with her. All has been forgotten, and he shall not even notice you now," Anne said, with a glance to her growing belly.

Elizabeth touched it as though shielding the child from judgment. "I am eager for this child to be born."

"You wouldn't think so after what you just saw your sister go through," Anne said under her breath.

"Perhaps not. But what woman is eager for childbirth?"

They reached the door to the bedchamber of the little prince.

One of the nursemaids eyed the pair of them suspiciously, as though they might be here to snatch the baby and run. Elizabeth gave a smile to the cross woman.

She peered over the crib, marvelling at the tiny creature inside. He did indeed have Jane's colouring. The blond hair and fair skin, but there was something strikingly Tudor about him.

His eyes opened to reveal a piercing blue colour.

"What pretty eyes," she was driven to comment.

"All babies have blue eyes," Anne said, unimpressed.

"I don't know about that," Elizabeth said. "Shall we place a wager?"

A *tsk* from one of the nursemaids. She held back a laugh. These must have been nuns in a previous life.

"What a bonny prince. I hope you continue to grow good and strong like your father," she said and then, with the customary curtsy one might give to the heir of England, she left the room with Anne.

"Now I must see my sister. Have you spoken to her yet?"

Anne nodded. "She is still unwell. Hurting, no doubt, but that is to be expected. Hopefully, she will be better to sit up by the time of the christening. All the ambassadors and foreign dignitaries will want to pay their respects. They are buying up half of London of its gold and treasures as we speak, while their masters send over gifts.

"It shall be like a holiday for months if that is the case," Elizabeth said.

"Hopefully, it shall never stop," Anne said in a wistful sort of way.

Jane was in her bed, bundled up in furs. As she approached, Elizabeth saw the blue tinge in her lips and had to stop herself from gasping.

Her sister looked half dead. Around her, everyone was chattering excitedly. Those who had been there were eagerly retelling the story of how the prince was born.

Then Jane stirred, as if sensing someone was watching her.

Her eyes opened and seemed to take a moment to focus on Elizabeth's face, but she smiled.

"Sister, I was wondering where you were."

Elizabeth curtsied as she should and approached rather timidly.

"You are...awake, I see." She couldn't say a lie right now. She did not look well, but that was hardly seeming to concern anyone else. "I must congratulate you on your success."

"Thank you, everyone has been saying the same," Jane said, looking away from her to the bed coverings above as if seeing something of interest.

"You are well? Someone is looking after you?" Elizabeth said at last.

"Yes, everyone has been most kind. They say Edward is strong and happy in the nursery. I couldn't ask for more. I shall recover soon. It is just that I lost so much blood when I gave birth, but with a few days of rest I shall be back on my feet. You will see," Jane said, as though she was trying to convince herself.

Elizabeth found that hard to believe right now.

"The king was so good to me. He said that I was his

dearest love and took the effort to reassure me that the next baby would come easier, by the grace of God. It was thus for his mother," Jane continued.

By now Elizabeth could feel her expression darkening. How could the king even mention that at this time? Was it not enough that he had his son? She knew that one son in the cradle was not enough to secure the dynasty, but it felt insensitive of him to even say such a thing.

Anne, seeming to sense her agitation, put a hand on her shoulder.

"Perhaps her grace wishes to rest," Anne said.

Jane nodded. "Yes, I am tired. Thank you for the part you played in helping me. I shall not forget it."

Elizabeth pressed a kiss to her sister's hands. They felt cold despite the warmth in the room.

It was only women who were visiting her now primarily. Over the next few days, Jane did seem to improve somewhat. She was even able to sit up on the third day.

The christening ceremony was underway, and the size of the court swelled. Everyone wanted to be there for the momentous occasion, even on such short notice. Many had been on standby, of course.

The king, however, was fearful that too many people would bring contagion into the palace and limited the number of people. All those who wanted to attend had to apply for permission, and everyone was vetted by a doctor to swear that they were not ill.

The Lady Elizabeth, only three years old, would be carried by Elizabeth's brother, Edward Seymour, in the procession. Lady Mary would receive her brother at the font. The king was being generous to his daughters now that he had a son. He was also parading his heirs.

Her family had been certain that he would not wish to include Lady Elizabeth in this, but it seemed that he had other plans. The girl was undeniably his. With her flaming red hair and temper, it was hard to imagine that someone else had fathered Anne Boleyn's child.

A large dais was constructed so that everyone could get a better view of the baby being christened.

Elizabeth sat waiting by her sister's side, so everything she had heard was second-hand, but she relayed the story as accurately as possible.

Jane did not seem to be improving, though she had been eating a rich diet of meat and sauces. Sweets and cakes were brought to her as she needed. She had grown so thin that Elizabeth thought this was a good thing.

Elizabeth held her up as they dressed her in the heavy royal robes lined with ermine. Her sister was dazzling in a gown of white with gold Tudor roses embroidered throughout it. Her hair had been washed and brushed, let loose down her back as she sat in the great bed of estate.

All signs of the birth, from the pallet bed to the dirty sheets, were gone.

The dark panelling of the room had disappeared to be replaced with brilliant tapestries depicting biblical scenes, primarily of the Virgin Mary with her son. But unlike the Madonna, her sister had suffered the travails of childbirth and was not nearly as serene.

The king arrived, a kiss to his wife and a nod of his head to Elizabeth. He took a seat on a grand chair under the cloth of estate and they began processing in.

"How are you, my love?" he said, but his eyes were focused not on her but on the gifts being brought in, as though he were calculating the value. He felt vindicated by his decision to marry her now and his actions against the rebels in the north.

Many of his advisers had urged him to caution, but he refused to listen to them, claiming that as the head of the church he knew right from wrong.

Elizabeth watched with some trepidation as person after person bowed to the royal pair. Prince Edward lay at her feet, wrapped in his swaddling bands, fast asleep after a hearty meal with the wet nurse.

He was a sweet baby with plump rosy cheeks.

She was not anxious about his survival, even though that was all anyone was focused on.

∽

The festivities were over and the king was busy putting together a small tournament in honour of his son, but Elizabeth, needing rest, retired to Austin Friars with her children and husband.

"Your feet are so swollen," Gregory noted one evening as they sat in bed side by side. He had not properly shared her bed in quite some time, as it was unsafe to lie with her while she was pregnant, but he often still slept by her side or joined her for conversation in the evening.

"I was on my feet too much," Elizabeth admitted. "I shall try to take better care of myself. We have gotten through this, and now I can rest."

He seemed serious as he spoke. "And if you are not more careful with yourself, I will see to it that you are locked up somewhere."

"I will break free," she said. "I cannot be held down for long." She winked. "What a wife you have been saddled with. I am sure all your friends drink to commiserate with you."

"They toast to my good fortune. Next summer I want you to meet my good friend Thomas Saddler. He was my tutor and fostered me for a time. Taught me a lot of what I know."

"I shall be happy to meet him. Especially if that means traveling away from court." She almost confessed to him how disgusted she was by everything at court, but thankfully she held back.

"And what of our plans for your lying-in? Do you want to set up your chamber here at Austin Friars or return to the country? And a wet nurse? I discovered that there isn't a shop one gets one from," he said.

She considered for only the briefest of moments before saying she would much rather travel back to the country.

"We can spend a quiet Easter together, for that would be when my baby is due if I calculated it correctly," she said, adding up the days in her mind. "I shall send out the chamberlain to look into potential families that would be suitable."

Gregory nodded. "Whatever you wish."

"I wish you were always so amenable," Elizabeth said under her breath.

"Did you say something?"

"No," she said, lying back. "I am tired now. Will you sleep here tonight or in your own room?"

"I'll let you rest without me crowding the bed," he said, rising from his spot, but not before kissing her forehead.

She smiled. "I never complained."

"But I could see how you longed to stretch out. Not to worry. I shall have you make it up to me."

"Oh? How so?"

"I want to see you rising from your childbed with a plump infant in your arms."

"I'll do my best," she said with a stretch and a yawn.

∽

Elizabeth was dreaming of running around Wolf Hall searching for a button she had lost, when a shake on her shoulder woke her.

She nearly screamed seeing Gregory's face there, illuminated only by a single candle.

"Elizabeth, you must wake," he said urgently.

"What is it? Is it the children? A fire?" She pushed back the covers.

"Your sister has taken ill."

"What?"

She was on her feet now but unsure what to do first. She wasn't dressed. She couldn't just run over to the palace either.

"The doctors are seeing her now. My father sent me a message. You are to come at once. She would wish to see you."

"She asked for me?"

"No...she cannot. The fever has made her barely lucid. But I know you would wish to be by her side. I assume you wouldn't forgive me for not letting you go to her side."

"Alice! Come help me dress," Elizabeth called out to her maid, who had just walked in. She too seemed like she had been shaken out of sleep.

"Yes, milady. What gown?"

"It doesn't matter, just not black. I don't want to scare my sister into thinking I am already mourning her loss," she said, whipping around the room and gathering what she thought she would need. Her headdress and cap were discarded on the dressing table.

"I'll leave you to get dressed and make sure the barge is ready to take us to court. Don't let yourself become too flustered. Think of our child too," Gregory said.

Elizabeth rolled her eyes but did try to take him to heart. The poor babe in her belly was likely to be born with a cross disposition at this point.

∽

Elizabeth was huddled into her furs as the boatmen rowed her and Gregory back to court. He kept a hand around her as though to steady her, and she did not push him away. It felt nice to feel like she had support.

"Has my brother been informed?"

"I suppose so."

"Why did he not send for me?"

"I don't know," Gregory said. "Perhaps he knew that someone else would have told you."

"He's been strange ever since I married you," she said.

"No, I don't think it is that. I think he feels he is a man on the rise. He is the uncle to the future king of England," Gregory said. "It would be enough to make any man develop a big head."

"I'll have to knock him down a peg or two. He should be taking care of his family, not planning some grandiose future." She was frowning.

Since they were little, Edward could be selfish and interested in himself, but they had always been close. Or she thought they were.

Would it surprise her now if he merely saw his sisters as stepping-stones to a greater future for himself? No, it shouldn't, but this would sting just the same.

∽

Jane was not conscious when she entered the room. Beads of sweat were forming on her forehead and her head moved from side to side.

A nurse was dipping a piece of linen in a basin of water and wiping her face, but it seemed to do nothing.

"Where are the doctors?" Elizabeth asked the quiet room. The faces of her sister's attendants were downcast. No one seemed to want to meet her eyes. Some were drying tears.

The king rose from his seat.

"Lady Elizabeth, your sister has caught childbed fever. The doctors have done all they can. It is in God's hands now."

"Your Grace." Elizabeth dropped into a deep curtsy. "Forgive me, I had not seen you."

He invited her to rise. "Your sister has had the best of care. I am sorry, for she was a true wife to me."

"God may yet bless her," Elizabeth said in a half whisper as she approached.

Jane's skin seemed nearly translucent, but her cheeks were flushed red from her fever.

She clutched her sister's hand as the tears came. She was unable to hold them back. A heavy hand lay on her shoulder. The king's. She looked up and saw that his face was wet with his own tears. Her heart softened for him. Perhaps his love for her sister was real.

Elizabeth stayed the whole day with her, helping the nurses spoon broth into her parched mouth.

At last Edward came, looking truly sorry and stressed.

"Should you be here, sister?"

Elizabeth glared at him. "I can be here if I wish. She was not only my sister but my queen as well. We owe her this much at least. She should not be cared for by the hands of strangers if these are to be her last moments."

He bowed his head in shame. "I am sorry."

"What do those words mean now? They can help no one." She shrugged off his hand.

"Elizabeth, please do not be angry with me," he said, his tone piously weak.

"How can I not be? You have been so focused on yourself and all that you might gain that you could not care for your own sister."

"That is unfair of you to say. What could I do? I am no doctor."

"No, but you might have shown her some care and concern. She felt so alone and so afraid of failure. She felt the pressure everyone was placing on her. Who could have withstood it for so long?"

He remained silent but did not leave.

Out of the corner of her eyes Elizabeth saw Archbishop Cranmer appear in the rooms. She felt as though history was repeating itself. She stood to her feet, as though ready to prevent him coming closer. She acted as though he was the angel of death himself, come to take her sister away.

Jane was too far gone to ever recover. That much was clear. But Elizabeth still stood in his way, her back straight, daring him to order her to move aside.

It was Edward's touch on her elbow that distracted her.

"Let him pass, Elizabeth," he urged her. "There is

nothing we can do for her now. Let her pass on with heaven's grace."

Elizabeth stifled a sob but let him embrace her.

Cranmer moved past them. He was sombre as he performed the last rites over her.

Jane muttered something in her feverish dreams, which he seemed to have taken as agreement that she was passing on in Christ, asking him to forgive her, the sins she had committed.

The days blended together. Elizabeth was often forced to go lie down and rest herself as she stayed by her sister's side, praying and hoping she would improve.

Sometimes it seemed like it would work, and there were a few days when it seemed like she might improve. Jane would drift out of her stupor and ask for Edward, and then for her husband, but by the time they came to her side she was gone again. They brought the baby to her often in an effort to cheer her spirits, but to no avail.

The struggle went on for a few more days before Jane breathed her last.

"Sweetheart, come away now. They must prepare her for burial," Gregory said in her ear.

Elizabeth found that her tears were spent.

Was God so cruel that he would take Jane away at the height of her triumph?

What had gone wrong? What could they have done?

Some logical part of her knew that there was nothing that could be done. These things just happened. They were fate.

A day later, Gregory came to her, sitting beside her side.

"They are planning the burial. Will you be well enough to be the chief mourner? They want to know."

Elizabeth looked out the window at the grey autumn sky. Who was this "they"?

"I will. It is my duty."

He seemed taken aback by the emotionless way in which she spoke. She did not blame him, but she needed to embrace this misery she felt. She would eventually come out of it. This intense sadness that enveloped her.

∽

The royal tailor came to fit her for a new gown of royal blue, the colour of mourning for the English. Over the top she would wear a dark blue cloak. The dull clothing suited her mood.

As they processed from the palace to the church for her sister's internment, she walked with her back straight as a rod, her face impassive in its stony expression.

She watched as the officers of her sister's household broke their staves of office over the coffin. Thus ending their allegiance to her.

Elizabeth knew that she would never forget her sister. She would never forget her duty to her. She would do her best to watch over the son she had left behind. If they let her, that was.

Gregory told her later that the king had entered a grief so great that the doctors worried for his sanity. He swore he would never marry again. He swore that Jane was the greatest love of his life and now he was a broken man.

∼

Cromwell suggested that Gregory and she return to the country. It was clear to him that she was unwell and needed to recover. The court was no place for a mourning pregnant woman.

She travelled back with her children. This time they seemed to pick up on the fact that something was wrong. They sat quietly for the most part. Henry thought Margery was fun enough to play with now that she could talk to him, and he took on the role of being an older brother, telling her stories and making up games for them.

Elizabeth would have loved to join in, but her mind was on her sister. The occasional moments of sarcasm that would escape her.

She allowed Gregory to send out for a wet nurse, a gentlewoman among their neighbours. He brought her a few options, and after a few interviews she settled on Sarah Thompson, daughter of an impoverished knight. She had a five-month-old son thriving in his nursery. She was recently widowed and needed the income and security being a nursemaid would provide. It did not seem to bother her that she would be serving a Cromwell. Many in the country hated the Cromwells; they had become the scapegoat for everyone's problems. From the weather to the poor harvest. Cromwell had become a byword for villainy. This was not her husband. He was gentle and kind when he wanted to be, but his father was ruthless and everyone seemed to think the devil must be at work for the Cromwells to have risen so high. He stood for greed, betrayal, and all sorts of sins.

It amused Elizabeth to think of how the king had gotten away with everything by simply blaming his ministers. There was something wrong about this. She felt a pang of pity for Cromwell, who was merely doing his master's bidding no matter the cost, even offering up his very soul.

She picked a room facing the orchard for her lying-in. The scent of apple blossoms might drift through the open window, and the thought brought a smile to her face.

As her own belly grew and the winter snows melted away, the pain in her heart over Jane's loss lessened and she found she could laugh again and join in games with her children.

To Gregory she was kinder. Deciding that despite everything he was still her husband and he had given her the greatest gift, her children. She enjoyed hearing about how the little prince was thriving in his nursery. Her own baby was giving her great kicks. He seemed eager to come out to greet the world. Gregory had asked her if she was frightened after witnessing what her sister went through, but she shrugged.

"What will be will be," she said, completely resigned to her fate. Nothing she did now could change it.

She bid her children and household farewell. They would still bring Margery in to see her, as she was still so young, but Henry would have to wait at least a month before seeing her again.

In the past she had dreaded confinement in the darkened room with nothing to look at but her relics and tokens of good luck, but now she welcomed the chance to sit in quiet contemplation. She wanted nothing to do with the outside world for a while.

The king, ever duplicitous, was speaking of siring other heirs. Elizabeth wondered what her brother's reaction would be, for she knew he still took the king at his word. Would he be shocked? Personally, she had not believed the king when he cried out over his heartbreak. She remembered Aske. She remembered the countless pardons with the king's seal and how those who received them ended up as rotting corpses hanging from every tree and rafter in the north.

So Elizabeth knew, even as she took her first steps into the dark chamber, the king's ambassadors were journeying across Europe with urgent missives in their satchels. The door creaked shut behind her, and she was in darkness.

Which eligible maiden would dare wed this king next?

AUTHOR'S NOTE

Elizabeth Seymour would go on to live primarily in the country following the death of her sister. After King Henry VIII's disastrous fourth marriage that ended in divorce, Thomas Cromwell fell from favour and was executed. As a traitor, all of his wealth reverted back to the crown. Eventually, Gregory was granted the title of Baron Cromwell, as well as lands once held by his father, and served in Parliament.

Elizabeth and he would go on to have five children together and were known for having a happy marriage. They rose to greater prominence once Prince Edward took the throne following the death of King Henry VIII in 1547. Unfortunately, in 1551 Gregory would die of the sweating sickness, leaving Elizabeth a widow for the second time. She would eventually remarry three years later. Her two older brothers, Edward and Thomas, never managed to get along. They would both die as traitors in the tower, by the order of their nephew, King Edward VI.